No Turning
Back

Cedar River Daydreams

 1 • New Girl in Town
 2 • Trouble with a Capital "T"
 3 • Jennifer's Secret
 4 • Journey to Nowhere
 5 • Broken Promises
 6 • The Intruder
 7 • Silent Tears No More
 8 • Fill My Empty Heart
 9 • Yesterday's Dream
10 • Tomorrow's Promise
11 • Something Old, Something New
12 • Vanishing Star
13 • No Turning Back
14 • Second Chance
15 • Lost and Found
16 • Unheard Voices
17 • Lonely Girl
18 • More Than Friends

Other Books by Judy Baer

• Paige
• Adrienne
• Dear Judy, What's It Like at Your House?

No Turning Back

Judy Baer

BETHANY HOUSE PUBLISHERS
MINNEAPOLIS, MINNESOTA 55438

All scripture quotations are taken from *The Everyday Bible, New Century Version*, copyright © 1987, 1988 by Word Publishing, Dallas, Texas 75039. Used by permission.

Cover illustration by Brett Longley,
Bethany House Publishers staff artist.

No Turning Back
Judy Baer

Library of Congress Catalog Card Number 91–73493

ISBN 1–55661–216–8

Published by Bethany House Publishers
A Ministry of Bethany Fellowship, Inc.
6820 Auto Club Road, Minneapolis, Minnesota 55438

Printed in the United States of America

For Joni

who chose me as her mentor

JUDY BAER received a B.A. in English and Education from Concordia College in Moorhead, Minnesota. She has had over nineteen novels published and is a member of the National Romance Writers of America, the Society of Children's Book Writers and the National Federation of Press Women.

Two of her novels, *Adrienne* and *Paige*, have been prizewinning bestsellers in the Bethany House SPRINGFLOWER SERIES (for girls 12–15). Both books have been awarded first place for juvenile fiction in the National Federation of Press Women's communications contest.

". . . if Christ is in you,
then the Spirit gives you
life, because Christ made
you right with God."

Romans 8:10

Chapter One

"I can't believe that school starts tomorrow," Binky McNaughton moaned. The entire gang, including Binky, her brother Egg, Todd Winston, Jennifer Golden and Lexi Leighton had all gathered at Lexi's home to commiserate the beginning of the new school year.

Binky alternated between complaining and stuffing food into her mouth. "I wanted summer to go on forever." She stared cross-eyed at a nacho covered with cheese. "We had so much fun, didn't we?"

"The recycling project was great," Egg agreed.

"And the tennis tournament!" Todd leaned back with a satisfied smile. "That was a real success."

"I think meeting Holly Agnew, the tennis star, was the most exciting thing I did all summer," Lexi announced.

"I don't want to see it end," Binky wailed. "I'm not ready."

"You'll never be ready, Binky," Egg pointed out matter-of-factly, as he plucked another piece of fudge from the plate in front of him.

Binky flung herself backward against the sofa. "Just think. We're going to be juniors! Doesn't that sound *old*?"

"Not to me," Jennifer retorted. "It's about time. I think this school thing has dragged on for too long already. It's taken forever to get this far!"

Just then, Benjamin Leighton wandered into the living room. He glanced at his sister's friends before making a beeline for the food on the coffee table. He popped a piece of fudge into his mouth and smiled blissfully. "Yummmm, Lexi. You and Todd made good fudge."

"What are you up to, Ben?" Jennifer asked.

"Waiting," Ben said.

"Aren't you doing anything else? Just waiting?"

Ben had grown taller over the summer, and his silky dark hair shagged lazily over his almond-shaped eyes. "I'm waiting for school to start," he said. His face split in a grin. "I'm going to the Academy."

Ben, who suffered from Down's syndrome, loved going to the Academy for the Handicapped. Over the summer he'd turned into a charming, outgoing little boy who was confident of his abilities.

"Ben, I do believe you're a foot taller than you were last spring." Egg stood beside Ben and measured the boy's head against his chest.

"I'm getting strong too." Ben curled his arm to make a muscle.

"And tan. You must play outside a lot."

"I play with my bunny. My teacher said that Bunny could come to school this year and be our class mascot. Isn't that great?" Ben threw them a high-wattage smile.

Lexi suppressed a grin. When Ben was born, she'd worried that he'd never be like other people. Now, after all these years, she'd learned that Ben *wasn't* like other people. In many ways, he was much, much better.

Ben took another piece of fudge and stuffed it into his mouth. "Gotta go," he mumbled through the chocolate. "Bunny's waiting." Without turning around, he gave a cheerful wave over his left shoulder.

"Humpft!" Jennifer reached for another nacho and then settled herself on the couch near Binky. "He's the first person I've met in a long time who's anxious for school to start. Maybe the public school could learn something from the Academy." She paused for a moment. "Or maybe I belong there."

Jennifer was always frustrated with school. She had dyslexia and classes were very difficult for her. Lexi looked at her sympathetically. "You're going to have a good year this year, Jennifer. I know you will."

A smile brightened Jennifer's face. "Of course it really did help meeting with a tutor and attending summer school. I'm so far ahead in some of my classes that I'm probably going to get better grades than any of you."

"Hey, no fair," Egg protested.

"You could have gone to summer school too, Egg," Jennifer said slyly.

Egg shook his head emphatically. "No, thanks. I was too busy."

"Crushing cans and driving people crazy," Binky pointed out.

"Think about it guys," Todd said. "We're going to be juniors. We're finally going to get some respect around school. All those freshmen and sophomores are going to look up to us."

"Yeah, and I'm going to be a senior," Egg said,

puffing out his chest and thrusting his chin in the air. "I'm *really* going to get some respect."

Binky snorted. "Not likely."

"I'm looking forward to getting back into the Emerald Tones," Lexi said. "Are we going on another tour this year?"

"Mrs. Waverly's been talking about it," Todd said. "I don't know what her final decision is going to be. Maybe we can go somewhere interesting for a change. Someplace far away."

"I've heard of high school bands that play at the Super Bowl," Binky said hopefully.

"But we're a *singing* group, Binky."

"Oh, yeah." Binky batted the heel of her hand against her forehead. "Cancel that comment. What a dope I am today. Going back to school has me all shook up."

"It won't be that bad," Egg consoled his sister. "At least not for me. I've got my job back on the *Cedar River Review*."

"So do we," Todd said, glancing at Lexi. "We're going to do the photography again. Mrs. Waverly said that Lexi is the best caption writer they've ever had on the paper. Actually, I'm looking forward to school."

"Oh sure, you are," Binky pointed an accusing finger at him. "And I know why, too."

Todd's eyebrows quirked upward. "You do? Why?"

"Because you're going to be the quarterback on the football team. You'll be a big athletic hero this fall. Everybody's crazy about the quarterback."

"I am looking forward to it. It's going to be a real challenge."

"It seems we all have something to look forward to," Lexi agreed. "Egg, aren't you going to be team manager again?"

"They couldn't do it without me."

Jennifer turned to Lexi with a scowl. "How come you're so cheerful? What is it that you're looking forward to this year?"

"You haven't figured it out by now?" Lexi pretended to act surprised. "Our family has lived in Cedar River for an entire year! Finally I don't feel like the *new* girl in town anymore. I know the names of all the teachers and a lot of the kids in school. I don't get lost in the hallways anymore, and best of all, I have friends. Last fall was scary for me—coming to this new place, having left my friends behind. This year I'll be going to school with people I know and care about."

"You've been here an entire year, huh, Lexi?" Egg looked thoughtful. "I guess now instead of calling you the 'new girl,' we'll have to start calling you the 'old girl.' "

"Thanks for nothing!" Lexi pretended to punch Egg in the arm.

"You guys can be excited if you want to be," Jennifer said gloomily, "but I don't like it. I don't want school to start." She plopped her elbows on her knees and cupped her chin in her hands. She stared blankly at the rug.

It was a long time before Jennifer spoke. "I wonder if Peggy Madison is playing on the girls' basketball team this year. Has she said anything?"

"Peggy told me she has tryouts tomorrow after school," Lexi answered. "She's a little nervous about it. I've seen her out in her driveway shooting hoops."

"Peggy's good," Binky said confidently. "She'll make it. Besides that, she's tall. Now, if I were going out for the basketball team, I'd have a right to be nervous." Binky was so tiny, she was sometimes mistaken for a junior high student. Once she was so insulted, she threatened to put a frosted streak in her hair to make herself look older. Fortunately, Lexi had been able to talk her out of that.

"You know, I think there's something weird going on between Chad and Peggy," Egg announced out of the blue.

Lexi and Todd exchanged a knowing glance. The rest of the gang still didn't know about Peggy's pregnancy during the previous school year. They'd promised Peggy that they would tell no one. It was Peggy's story and hers alone to tell.

"I wonder why they broke up," Binky said. "They made such a perfect couple."

"I don't think Chad wanted to break up," Egg said with some authority.

"What makes you say that?" Jennifer asked.

"Because of the way he acted after Peggy and her parents went to Arizona to stay with her uncle. It sounds funny, but he acted kind of depressed."

"What do you know about being depressed?" Binky asked sarcastically.

Egg glared at her. "Plenty, having you for a sister." Binky gave a little huff as Egg continued.

"In health class we were reading about depression. Chad used to complain that he wasn't sleeping at night. Sometimes he'd be late for school, because if he *did* fall asleep, he had a hard time waking up again."

It was obvious from Egg's expression that he'd given this a lot of thought. "Do you remember how much Chad loved pizza? We went out for pizza one night. He ate a half a piece and left the rest on his plate."

"Maybe he had a stomachache," Binky offered.

"I don't know. Maybe." Egg shrugged. "All I do know is that he's lost his sense of humor."

"You can't joke around with Chad Allen anymore," Jennifer agreed. "Every time you try, he thinks you're picking on him."

Binky's expression grew interested. "That's true! I've never thought about it that way before. Chad *doesn't* seem very happy. It's as though he moves through the day like a puppet on a string instead of like a real person."

"He and Peggy were close for a long time," Jennifer said. "It isn't surprising that he'd feel badly about their breaking up."

"Frankly, I can't believe it happened," Binky said. "They seemed so serious about each other. I thought they were really in love."

Lexi remained quiet. Todd, across the room, didn't speak either. Neither wanted give away the fact that Peggy had had Chad's baby and given it up for adoption.

Lexi bit the inside of her lip as the conversation continued. She knew that after the baby, Peggy had decided never to have premarital sex again. When Chad had tried to force Peggy to have sex with him, they'd had a terrible fight. Lexi knew deep in her heart that Peggy would never go back to Chad after what had happened between them. She was also sure

Chad was still in love with Peggy, and was hurt by her rejection.

As the conversation in the room swirled about her, Lexi thought about the things that Peggy had told her. Chad didn't seem to understand that forcing a girl to have sex was wrong. He assumed that since they'd had sex before the baby, he could demand it now.

Lexi was relieved when her friends decided to break up for the evening and go home. It was uncomfortable to think about Peggy and Chad and what had transpired between them.

"I have to go," Jennifer announced. "I need to go through my closet and pick out clothes for school tomorrow."

"Me too," Binky chimed in. "No doubt Minda Hannaford will be taking notes on what everyone is wearing for her first fashion column in the *River Review*."

"We don't care what Minda thinks of us!" Jennifer insisted. "She'd hate us even if we came to school wearing the crown jewels!"

"Well, I care what she thinks," Binky said.

Egg primped and preened and pulled his collar up. "Of course I have to know what I'm going to wear because all the girls will be mobbing me as soon as I walk through the school door."

"Of course," Binky echoed. "That happens every year, doesn't it?"

Egg gave her a warning look through squinted eyes.

Binky reached for the last of the nachos and stuffed the crumbs into her mouth.

"You're going to get fat, Binky," Egg chanted. "I'm sure you're fatter than you were last spring. You'd better quit eating like that."

Binky crossed her eyes at her brother. "I am not. I'm just a growing girl. Mother says I'm 'filling out.'"

"Yeah, right," her brother taunted. "That's what happens to balloons when you blow them up, Binky. Pretty soon you're going to look like a balloon—a lead balloon. Too heavy to float."

"Leave her alone, Egg," Jennifer said. "Binky looks good. She's been scrawny all her life. She could use five pounds."

"Yeah," Binky turned to her brother. "See? Jennifer thinks I look good."

"You're getting fat, Binky. There's no two ways around it."

Jennifer shook her head and waved at Lexi and Todd. "See you guys tomorrow. Thanks for the food."

"Right. The fudge was delicious." Binky picked up a piece and popped it into her mouth before her brother could comment. She made a face at him. "Don't you dare."

"You always think you know what I'm going to say, Binky," Egg said. "Well, you don't. It's rude to interrupt someone when they're about to speak."

"What you were about to say *was* rude, Egg. That's why I didn't want to hear it."

As the two left the Leighton's and walked down the sidewalk, their conversation faded. All Lexi could hear was Binky's squealing and fuming as Egg teased her.

"Those two will never quit bickering, will they?" Lexi asked.

"Not for a few years, anyway," Todd said with a laugh. "Maybe when they're eighty and in a nursing home. I doubt it will happen before then." Todd slipped an arm around Lexi and gave her a squeeze. "Are you thinking about Chad and Peggy?" he asked softly.

"Yes. It was hard not to say something when everyone was discussing their relationship. I really do worry about both of them."

Todd nodded somberly. "I don't blame you. Frankly, I don't think Chad has come to grips with the fact that he's a father or that his baby was given up for adoption."

Lexi shot Todd a questioning look. "What do you mean by that?"

"I don't think he's realized exactly what's happened. After all, Peggy went away to have her baby and give it up for adoption. Chad never saw the child. He knows in his head there's a baby out there that's his, but I'm not sure his heart is convinced of it. Besides, I think Chad has a lot of guilty feelings about Peggy and the baby."

"You've talked to him about it?"

"I've tried. Chad has a hard time opening up to anyone. It seems his family doesn't like to discuss anything unpleasant. No one has helped him to work things out."

"You mean they're ignoring the fact that Chad fathered a baby?"

Todd nodded, his expression serious. "His family told him to forget about the baby, that 'boys will be boys.' His dad said that getting pregnant was Peggy's problem, not Chad's."

"It takes two to make a baby!" Lexi sputtered indignantly.

"His folks have an old-fashioned, unrealistic point of view. You and I know that, but I don't think Chad does. He believes what his family's told him. He told me that none of this would have happened if *Peggy* had been more careful. He believes that the pregnancy was Peggy's fault. Now he's upset that she doesn't want to date him anymore."

"How awful!" Lexi exclaimed.

"Chad is one mixed up guy, Lexi. I don't know how to help him."

"You shouldn't have to help him, Todd," Lexi retorted indignantly. "Chad should be going to a counselor. His family should see to that."

"But his family thinks the issue is over and done."

"How irresponsible!"

"Worse yet, Chad still wants Peggy back. He wants to pretend the past never happened. The pregnancy. The date rape. Everything."

"What can he be thinking about?"

"Himself, obviously. He certainly isn't thinking of Peggy. I offered to help Chad," Todd said. "I told him I'd talk to him about anything, anytime he wanted. That even if he woke up in the middle of the night, he could give me a call. I also told him my mom knew of some good counselors, that I could get the name of someone from her."

"What did Chad say about that?"

"He wouldn't accept my help. He was too proud and too ashamed. He didn't want me to talk to my mother. He said his dad would kill him if word ever got out about what happened."

"Oooooh, this makes me so mad!" Lexi stiffened, her shoulders rigid.

"I told him that if he wouldn't get help, he should at least date other girls. I thought if he found another girlfriend, it might help him to forget about Peggy."

"What did he say to that?"

"Chad doesn't want to date other girls. He only wants Peggy." Todd looked serious. "Egg was right, Chad is depressed. In fact, while we were talking, Chad actually cried."

"*Chad* cried?" Lexi's heart twisted with pain.

"It was as though his emotions were on a roller coaster. One minute he was angry, the next depressed, then he'd cry or rant and rave about how awful Peggy was treating him. It was pretty scary. He said he'd do anything to get Peggy back."

"But Peggy won't take *him* back."

"Then I don't know what's going to happen to Chad."

"Can't his parents see any of this?"

"I don't think Chad has ever really communicated his true feelings to his mother or father." Todd shrugged. "I don't know of many guys my age that do."

"You do," Lexi said softly.

"Yeah. My mom has always encouraged me to admit my feelings and not keep them bottled up inside. It works, too. Once I blow off a little steam or share my problems, things don't seem so bad anymore."

"If blowing off steam helps, and Chad isn't doing it, he must be like a volcano about to erupt," Lexi reasoned.

A trace of fear darkened Todd's eyes. "Don't say that, Lexi."

"What's wrong? You sound panicked."

"I just don't like thinking about Chad and his problems," Todd admitted. "He did something really scary in the locker room the other day. I've been worrying about him ever since. I didn't know who to tell. He said the world would be 'a better place' if he weren't living in it. That if he died, no one would miss him."

"You mean he's thinking of committing suicide?" Lexi gasped.

"He didn't say that in so many words, but that's what he implied. I know that's what he was thinking. I'm really worried about him, Lexi. He's not very stable. I think he could actually hurt himself if Peggy keeps turning him away. I don't want Chad to do anything stupid." Todd was quiet for a few minutes, then hauled himself off the couch and slowly headed for the front door.

They said good night and Lexi closed the door behind him. She moved listlessly into the living room and began to pick up the plates and napkins that were littered about. Chad Allen had never been a close friend to Lexi, but she didn't want to see him hurt. She stared out the window into the deepening dusk. What was in store for this new year at Cedar River High?

Chapter Two

Ben was already awake when Lexi's alarm clock rang the next morning. She could hear his off-key singing from the shower.

He came skidding out of the bathroom, wrapped in a fluffy towel as Lexi walked down the hallway.

"All done in there, Ben?"

"Yup. Ben's up early. I'm ready to go to the Academy."

"I hope you're not going like that, Ben," Lexi teased, pointing at the over-sized towel.

Ben made a face at her. "Funny, Lexi, funny." Then he smiled. "Mom's making pancakes for breakfast!" He scooted off down the hall.

Thirty minutes later, Lexi met her little brother at the kitchen table. He was eyeing a stack of pancakes covered with melted butter and syrup.

"Can you eat all those, Ben?" Lexi asked, already knowing the answer.

"I need my strength," he retorted, as he dug into the stack.

"I've never seen anyone so excited to start school as your brother, Lexi. How do you feel today?" Lexi's mother asked.

Lexi shrugged. "All right, I guess. But it's been a good summer. I hate to see it end."

"Time flies by," Mrs. Leighton sighed. "My children are growing up. Look at you two. Only two years from now and you'll be ready for college, Lexi."

"Me too?" Ben inquired.

"No siree, Ben." Mrs. Leighton gave her son a hug. "I'm keeping you here with me. You can't go off to school too."

"Okay!" Ben cheerfully turned back to his food.

Lexi glanced at the clock. "Todd's going to be here any minute." She'd eaten a pancake and had a glass of juice when she heard the horn of Todd's '49 Ford Coupe outside. "There he is. Gotta go!" She picked up her book bag, gave Ben a quick kiss on the top of his head and smiled at her mother. "See you tonight."

Todd had polished his car for the first day of school and it gleamed brightly in the sunlight. He looked handsome and ready for the new school year as well. His golden blond hair was slicked back and he wore a baby blue shirt that enhanced the color of his eyes.

The car was already full. Jennifer and Binky sat in the backseat, and Egg had taken the front seat with Todd.

As Lexi neared the car, Egg jumped out and held the door for her. "You can sit in front with us, Lexi," he announced.

"Thanks." Lexi was taken aback by Egg's clothes. He wore leopard-spotted Zubaz, one red sock and one blue, and his hi-tops were untied. His sweatshirt was a blinding purple, splashed with lightning bolts and footballs.

"Good morning—Egg," Lexi finally stammered. "New outfit?"

"Yeah. I should make a real hit on the first day of school, don't you think?"

There was no denying that. Lexi smiled weakly. "Just don't go into the library today, Egg."

"Why not?"

"Your outfit is too loud! You'll be kicked out for sure."

"Hah! Great, isn't it?"

Without another word, Lexi climbed into the car and turned around to peer into the backseat. Jennifer looked wonderful. Her hair was pulled back in a sleek ponytail and she wore an attractive denim dress with a wide red belt.

"You look super!" Lexi blurted.

Jennifer wrinkled her nose. "Maybe I can stun the teachers with my beauty. I can't seem to do it with my brains."

"How do you like my outfit, Lexi?" Binky asked brightly.

She wore a short black skirt and a black and white checked top. Her hair was swept on top of her head and fastened with a black and white checked barrette.

"Very nice, Binky. I like it a lot."

"Good. Me too." Binky settled against the seat, wearing a smile of satisfaction. "You look nice, too, Lexi. Is your outfit new?"

Lexi waved her hand. "Just something I sewed up a couple of weeks ago."

"You *made* that?" Binky's voice was charged with amazement.

Lexi wore a blue and black striped knit top and black stirrup pants. With leftover fabric from the top, she'd made a headband.

"You look like you just stepped out of the pages of a teen magazine," Binky said enviously. "And you made it yourself! I can't believe it. You'll have to teach me how to sew, Lexi."

"Anytime."

"Now that this mutual admiration society has held its meeting, can we get going?" Todd asked.

Lexi turned around in the seat. "You look nice too, Todd," she said. "Were you feeling a little left out?"

"No, I just want Egg to close the door so we can get moving."

"Take your time, Egg," Jennifer yelled from the back. "I don't want to get there any sooner than I have to. School . . . Yuck!"

"What would we do all day if we never went to school?" Todd asked. "And what could we make of our lives without an education?"

"Lexi could start her own fashion business. She's so good at designing and sewing clothes," Binky piped up. "Jennifer, you could work for her. How about that?"

"I wish I *could* design my own clothes," Lexi admitted. "But I couldn't start without some college courses in design and textiles."

"You mean you need to be a college graduate for that?"

"I don't suppose you have to," Lexi said, "but I'm sure it would help."

"That means I'll just have to stick it out," Jennifer

said, her tone resigned. "Actually, I'd like school if I didn't have so much trouble reading. I put off taking typing until this year because I dreaded trying to figure out how to keep my fingers and my brain co-ordinated." She shuddered. "It's going to be a nightmare, I just know it."

"Don't give up already. We're not even at the school yet," Egg reminded her.

"Oh yes we are," Todd said, turning the corner. "Here's the parking lot."

He dropped his passengers at the front door. "I'll see you in home room," he said. "I'm going to park at the far end of the lot."

Binky, Jennifer, Egg and Lexi all piled out of the car and into the building. The hallways were humming with activity. Voices were high-pitched, everyone chattering about summer vacation.

"Where's our home room, Lexi?" Binky asked.

"Mrs. Waverly's our home room teacher. That means home room must be the same place as it was last year."

The foursome found seats together near the front of the room. Egg threw his book bag on a fifth seat, saving it for Todd.

The High-Fives, including Minda Hannaford, Tressa and Gina Williams, and Rita Leonard were clustered at the back, giggling loudly and snapping their gum.

Tressa Williams was a tall redhead and past president of the High-Fives. Lexi didn't know Tressa or her sister Gina well, but she did know that they lived in a large six-bedroom Spanish-style ranch house. She also knew that the girls were confident, but often trouble-makers.

Rita Leonard was a tall blonde who usually wore thick black eye makeup and blood-red lipstick. Today she wore a denim skirt and a lightweight sweater, the same color as her lipstick.

It was Minda who stood out in the crowd, however. Her blonde hair was teased into a golden cloud around her head. She wore brightly colored floral tights and a long, oversized sweater. Minda was always concerned about the latest fashions and trends.

"Minda is fashion columnist for the school paper again," Egg whispered to Lexi.

She wasn't surprised. Minda was the most fashion conscious girl in school. There was really no one else for the job, even though Minda often played distasteful pranks in her column.

"That means another year of putting up with her hi-jinks," Egg groaned. "I'm not sure I can stand having her around the *Cedar River Review* layout room."

"You'll manage," Lexi assured her friend. "You always do."

Just then, Anna Marie Arnold and Matt Windsor walked into the room. Lexi waved enthusiastically to both of them.

"Anna Marie looks great," Binky whispered.

Binky was right. Even though she'd put on a few pounds since the last time Lexi had seen her, it was a relief to see Anna Marie looking so normal. She had battled with an eating disorder and had gone from very plump to very thin.

"And doesn't Matt look super?" Jennifer murmured in Lexi's ear.

"I'm anxious to hear how his summer was at Yellowstone Park."

Jennifer stood up and waved them over. "There're two seats over here."

Matt and Anna Marie joined the gang.

"Good to see you guys," Lexi remarked.

"Great tan!" Binky enthused.

"Love your hair cut," Jennifer added.

"So, how was Yellowstone?"

"Did you have fun traveling with your family?"

"I hear there was some excitement at the tennis tournament this summer."

The conversation leap-frogged from one topic to another, everyone talking at once. Matt had just finished telling a funny anecdote about his experiences in Yellowstone Park when Peggy and Chad appeared together in the home room doorway.

They were framed in the entrance for only a second before Peggy darted into the room and toward a seat near Lexi, leaving Chad standing alone on the other side of the room. Because there were no more available seats near the others, he was forced to sit at the back of the room near the High-Fives.

Peggy didn't say a word, keeping her head down and refusing to look Lexi in the eye. Even from across the room, Lexi could see the angry expression on Chad's face. She turned around to exchange a curious glance with Todd. Unfortunately, there was no time to talk.

Mrs. Waverly bustled into the room, carrying a stack of books, her pale blonde hair stacked high on her head and tipped slightly to the side. She took a pencil from her hair and rapped it on the top of her desk to call attention to the class.

"Here are your new schedules, people," Mrs. Waverly announced. "You'll need them to get around each day. Let's hand them out and then I'll answer any questions you might have." She then proceeded with a long list of announcements and instructions.

There was a spirited discussion about class officers. Nominations were taken from the floor. Names were to be posted in the hallway with the ballot box. Each student was given a ballot as they walked out the door to their next class. The rest of the morning was spent finding their way between classes, getting new books and assignments. It was noon before Lexi and her friends met again.

Lexi, Jennifer and Binky all went through the cafeteria line together. "I see Egg and Todd have saved a table for us," Jennifer pointed out. "We'd better get there before someone else takes our spot."

Lexi led the way to the table and sat down near Todd. Jennifer took a place across from her. Lexi lowered her head to give thanks silently.

Jennifer's lip curled as she looked down at her meal. "Look at this. School food. Can you believe it? It seems like only yesterday that we had to eat this stuff."

"Looks okay to me," Egg said, his fork poised between the tray and his mouth.

"Maybe you like mystery meat and leftover noodles," Jennifer retorted.

"How can it be leftover noodles? We haven't had school for three months," Egg responded.

Jennifer nodded. "No wonder they're so gross. Three-month-old noodles. Yuck!"

The others ignored the comment and continued to eat. After Todd pushed his tray away, he asked, "I wonder why we always have canned peaches? They must buy them by the truckload."

Lexi was about to reply when she noticed Peggy coming through the lunch line with her tray. She was headed for Lexi's table when Chad Allen caught her.

Peggy resisted, but he clung to her, forcing her to sit with him. Her face flushed and her lips trembled. She was near tears. Chad's expression was stormy as he spoke emphatically to Peggy.

Peggy's shoulders drooped and her head bowed. She didn't make any attempt to eat. Suddenly Peggy stood up, pushed her tray toward Chad and darted out of the lunchroom.

Lexi instinctively rose from her seat. "Excuse me, I'm going to the restroom."

In the hallway, Lexi looked quickly in both directions. At the far end of the corridor, she saw a flash of red hair disappear into one of the women's lavatories.

The restroom appeared empty, but Lexi could hear Peggy crying softly in one of the stalls. "Peggy, it's me, Lexi."

"Please go away. Leave me alone."

"Of course I'm not going to leave you alone," Lexi said soothingly. "Come out and tell me what's wrong."

"I can't. Please leave me alone."

"Come out and talk to me, Peggy. You can't lock yourself in there all day."

"You can't help me, Lexi. No one can."

"Maybe I can't, but I'm a good listener."

Slowly, the door opened and Peggy came out. Her eyes were swollen and red, her cheeks flushed, and her chest heaved with sobs. She was barely in control. Lexi reached out to rub Peggy's back in an effort to console her.

"You've got to calm down, Peggy. Take a deep breath. Now, tell me what happened. Did Chad hurt you?" Lexi asked, remembering Chad's firm hand on Peggy's arm in the lunchroom.

"We fight all the time, Lexi. It's horrible. Just horrible. I don't like fighting with anyone, especially Chad."

"What do you fight about?"

"He wants me to date him again, Lexi. He refuses to take no for an answer. He follows me everywhere and calls me constantly. He won't leave me alone."

"Oh, Peggy, I'm so sorry."

"I won't date him. I told him I wouldn't. Chad has disappointed me too badly. I can't go back to him. First the pregnancy, then the date rape. Now he denies all that has gone on. He wants me back. He wants things to be the way they were before the baby. He just won't listen. He acts as though he's obsessed. What am I going to do, Lexi?"

"Maybe he's really concerned about you, Peggy— but doesn't know how to express himself."

"He's changed, Lexi. He's not the same boy I used to know. His temper is much worse. He's always impatient and angry. We can't talk anymore. He has these mood swings. One minute he acts like he's happy and the next he's furious about something. I can't stand to be around him." Peggy drew another ragged breath. "And there's more . . . like what he told me today in the lunchroom."

"What did he say to you, Peggy?"

"He said he couldn't live without me. He told me he *won't* live without me."

An icy feeling grew in the pit of Lexi's stomach.

"Peggy, you have to tell someone about this. You can't carry this kind of burden around."

"Who can I tell? Who would understand? My parents are so happy I'm not dating Chad anymore, they wouldn't care what he says. They'd just say he's threatening me to get me back."

Lexi had no answer. The situation between Peggy and Chad was deteriorating rapidly.

The warning bell rang for their next class.

"Listen, Peggy," Lexi said encouragingly, "there's a football game tonight. Binky and I are going. Why don't you come with us? That way, if Chad comes around, we'll be able to protect you. We won't let him upset you. We can talk more about this, too. It'll help you to get out. Will you come?"

Peggy was silent for a moment, then nodded her head slowly. "It would be nice to spend some time with you. I don't want to be with Chad and I don't want to be home if he calls me."

"This is Todd's first game as varsity quarterback, you know."

"It's a big night then." Peggy smiled weakly. "I wouldn't want to miss it."

"What time should we pick you up?"

"I'll meet you at the game. I have basketball tryouts tonight." She rubbed the tears from her cheeks. "I hope to get back on the team, Lexi. I really love basketball. Besides that, it would keep me busy after school. I'd have an excuse to be somewhere that Chad wasn't."

"It's a good idea, Peggy. I hope you make it."

The second bell rang sharply and both girls glanced at the clock on the wall. "See you tonight, Peggy—at the game."

As Lexi walked down the rapidly emptying corridor, she said a little prayer for Peggy. Her friend's problem was getting more serious. *What is Peggy going to do?*

Chapter Three

"I'll get it," Lexi called when the doorbell rang. "I'm sure it's Binky." She hurried down the stairs and threw open the front door.

Binky stood on the porch, tapping her foot. "Well, are you ready to go? We have a long walk."

Lexi pulled the door shut behind her. "What an evening!"

Even Binky, who wasn't much of an outdoor person, had to agree. "It is beautiful. I love fall nights. Especially during football season."

Lexi tipped her head backward and allowed the crisp fall air to wash over her face. "I hope Todd plays well. He was nervous at school today."

"He's going to be great," Binky said confidently. "He's going to be the best quarterback Cedar River's ever had."

"That's what I told him. He just didn't quite believe me."

The two girls walked quickly. Soon they reached the Cedar River High football field. There were rows of bleachers lining both sides of the lush green field, illuminated by bright banks of light. The teams were on the field doing their warm-ups. Lexi could hear the huffs and grunts of the players as they went through their exercises.

The stands were already filling. Many people were carrying thermoses of hot chocolate, popcorn and blankets.

"Isn't it great out here?" Binky asked with genuine pleasure.

Lexi could only nod. It really was. The air was crackling with excitement. "There's always something especially thrilling about a football game, isn't there?"

"I never used to think so, but now that Egg has been trying to teach me about the game, I'm beginning to enjoy it more."

"Where is Egg?" Lexi looked around.

"Over there, acting like Mr. Bigshot." Binky pointed across the field.

Egg did look official, bustling about in his manager's uniform. He was moving equipment and water bottles around, making sure everything was in place for the start of the game.

"I know Egg would like to play football," Binky lowered her voice confidentially, "but he's so skinny. He'd probably get snapped in two."

"He's a good manager, though. Todd says so," Lexi consoled her.

"Todd always has nice things to say about everyone," Binky said. She stared out across the field. "Todd looks great in his uniform, doesn't he?"

"There's no way I can deny that," Lexi responded with a grin. "Those shoulder pads certainly do something for a guy."

"Yeah, and the smell of popcorn does something for me. I'm starving."

Lexi and Binky made their way to the concession stand where they each bought a large tub of buttered popcorn. They also bought the largest-size cola and asked for two straws so they could share.

Binky looked around. "Where's Peggy? I thought you said she was meeting us here tonight."

"She is. At least she said she was. She had basketball tryouts after school. We'll just have to watch for her and save her a place in the bleachers."

"I hope she makes the team." Binky's expression showed concern. "It might be hard after missing so much of last year's season, though."

"I've thought of that, too. The girl's basketball team was really doing well at the end of the year. I don't know what Peggy's chances are."

"I've heard some really tall girls are going out for the team. Do you think Peggy will be upset if she doesn't make it?"

"She'd be terribly disappointed if she didn't make the team." Lexi recalled the conversation she and Peggy had in the restroom at school that afternoon. She didn't need any more disappointments.

"Jerry Randall's here!" Binky pointed to a boy in the crowd. "He must have the night off at the Hamburger Shack."

"I see Anna Marie sitting by Todd's parents," Lexi said. "Even Matt Windsor came. And of course, the High-Fives," Lexi pointed to the cluster of girls near the top of the bleachers.

"They wouldn't miss a game," Binky pointed out. "All the boys are here!"

It was fun to wave and greet their friends as they made their way through the bleachers to a place at the top. Binky handed Lexi her popcorn and began digging in the backpack she had slung over one shoulder.

"What are you looking for now?" Lexi asked.

"My food." Binky retrieved a package of red licorice and a bag of powdered donuts. "I need some nourishment for the game." She also pulled out a large sack of sunflower seeds. "Do you think this will be enough to last?"

"Binky, I don't eat that much junk in a week!"

Binky looked at Lexi crossly. "You're no fun. Football games are for junk food." She dug happily into her popcorn. "And I'm going to eat it all."

Ignoring Binky, Lexi looked around again. It was odd that Peggy hadn't arrived yet. Perhaps they'd missed her in the crowd. Lexi stood up and turned to look over the back side of the bleachers toward the parking lot. She spotted Peggy, walking slowly and dejectedly. When a group of small boys ran by and bumped in to her, Peggy didn't even look up.

"Peggy! Over here! Here we are!" Lexi waved frantically. It took a moment to capture Peggy's attention. Her eyes were without expression. "Up here, Peggy. Come on up."

Peggy nodded and moved woodenly toward the bleachers.

"Is she coming?" Binky asked, intent on her food and the activity on the football field.

"Yes, but I think something's wrong."

"Why's that?"

"Because she looks terrible."

Binky stopped chewing long enough to frown. "Didn't she make the team?"

"I don't know. We'll just have to wait and find out."

Peggy mounted the steps to the top. As she made her way toward their seats, Lexi could tell that something was desperately upsetting Peggy. She sank down beside them and slumped wearily against the backboard of the bleachers.

"Well? What happened?" Binky demanded.

"I won't be a starter," Peggy said, her voice flat. "I missed too much time last year."

"But you made the team, didn't you?" Binky said.

"I should have been a starter. I would have been if I hadn't been gone last year. I missed too much." Her voice quivered. "The coach told me that after I left, some of the other girls he played in my place really improved. One of them is starting."

"Hey, don't feel so badly," Binky chirped. "This is only the beginning of the season. You don't know what's going to happen the rest of the year. You might be starting in a couple of weeks."

Lexi remained silent. Binky didn't understand how important it was for Peggy to be one of the five starters for the first girls' basketball game of the year. Only the best players got that opportunity, and Lexi knew that Peggy interpreted that to mean that she wasn't one of the best. Lexi put her hand on Peggy's arm. "Binky's right, Peggy. Just because you're not starting for the first game doesn't mean you won't be starting later in the season."

"The coach is angry with me, Lexi. He thinks that I abandoned the team to go to Arizona."

"Well, that's his problem, Peggy, not yours." Lexi knew the coach would eat his words if he knew the real reason Peggy had to go to Arizona. "All you can do now is show him that you're still a top player and that you should be starting with the rest of your teammates."

"I suppose you're right. I'll try my best. But don't worry about me, Lexi."

Lexi couldn't help being concerned.

Fortunately, the three girls were soon swept up in the excitement of the game. Cedar River players had never looked better. There was no doubt about it, Todd was a spectacular quarterback.

The Statue of Liberty play clinched it. The center hiked the ball to Todd who spun around. In the turn, he pretended to give the ball to the running back coming up the middle of the field. Then Todd fell back as if he were going to pass the ball. As he did, one of the halfbacks took the ball from him and ran a sweep around the field for a touchdown. Todd was left standing in the middle of the field, his arm in the air—like the Statue of Liberty.

It was a clever play that set the fans to calling Todd's name and cheering.

The girls hugged each other giddily at the end of the game. "It was soooo good," Binky squealed, "I almost forgot to finish my licorice. Are you going to talk to Todd tonight and tell him how wonderful he was?"

"He's going home with his parents. Maybe he'll call me later if he gets a chance."

"Cedar River has a new football hero!"

They all descended the bleachers and walked toward the street. Peggy had cheered up during the game and Lexi was pleased. She hated to see her friend in such a down mood.

Binky babbled happily about the game all the way to her corner. "Here's where I get off," she announced. "See you guys in school."

Lexi and Peggy watched Binky jog down the sidewalk toward her house. Then the two of them walked on in silence.

"I'll walk you to your door," Peggy offered as they neared the Leighton household.

"Good. You can come and sit on the steps with me for a while. It's such a beautiful evening, I hate to go inside." Lexi sat down on the top step and rested her elbows on her knees. She knew Peggy wanted to talk. "Want to talk?"

Peggy sighed and leaned against the porch railing. "I don't know if talking anymore will help, Lexi. I've talked to you so much about my pregnancy, about the baby, about Chad. What good has it done? I still can't forget about my baby and I can't make Chad leave me alone. Why can't he understand what I've been through? Why can't he let me put my life back together?"

"Chad doesn't see things the same way you do, Peggy. He's probably trying to put his life back together, too. Apparently his definition of that includes you."

Peggy shook her head emphatically. "I could never go on with my life and still continue my relationship with Chad. He'll have to accept that."

"It might take him awhile, Peggy."

"Maybe you're right." Peggy brushed her hand across her eyes and then stared at a flickering street light. "I really wonder sometimes, Lexi, if life is actually worth the hassle."

"Of course it is!" Lexi blurted, stunned by her friend's statement.

"It might be for you. You don't have a pregnancy and a furious boyfriend in your past. When I try to figure out what's gone wrong and how I can change it, I get all mixed up. I'm not sure that my life is ever going to be better, if I'll ever be happy again. Sometimes I think it might be easier just to end it all," Peggy went on, without emotion. "Then it would be all over. Nothing."

"That's not true!" Lexi was emphatic. "I don't believe that at all."

"What do you mean?"

"There's a verse in Hebrews that says that after death comes judgment. I don't believe there is *nothing* on the other side of life. As a Christian, I believe that death is not the end but a new beginning. If you believe in Jesus Christ as your Savior, death means entrance into heaven and eternity with God. People who commit suicide have to stand before Christ too. They will have to be judged as well."

"You mean God judges a person for taking his own life?"

"God has plans for our lives, Peggy. He doesn't want our lives cut short before His plan is completed."

"You do look at things in the most interesting way, Lexi," Peggy said with a puzzled expression.

Lexi took Peggy's hands in hers and held them tightly. "Life is precious, Peggy. It's a gift from God. Don't take that for granted. Don't let a misunderstanding with Chad make you think you should end your own life. You've got a chance to start over, Peggy. Take it."

Peggy gave Lexi a warm smile. "I didn't mean to scare you, Lexi. I know that life is worth living; that it's precious. I know that now more than ever, because I've given birth to a baby. It's a miracle. I realize that. When I get depressed I need friends like you. Thanks, Lexi, for being someone I can talk to."

"Anytime. You know that." Lexi reached out to give her friend a hug. When Peggy finally said good night, her step was lighter and she looked more confident. Still, Lexi was frightened for her. What would happen to Peggy and Chad? How would everything work out?

Chapter Four

Lexi left the house early the next morning for the Madisons. Peggy's mother met her at the back door.

"Good morning, Lexi. You look nice today."

"Thank you. Is Peggy still here?"

"Yes. She's a little slow this morning. I don't think she slept very well last night."

They exchanged an understanding look. It was obvious they both knew how troubled Peggy was, and felt equally helpless.

Peggy appeared in the kitchen doorway. "Lexi, what are you doing here?"

"I came to walk you to school. Are you ready?"

Peggy took a blueberry muffin from the basket on the table. "Sure. Let's go." She gave her mother a distracted wave. "See you tonight."

Peggy didn't speak as they stepped outside. Lexi wondered if she'd made a mistake coming to the house. Peggy didn't seem happy to see her. But then Peggy didn't seem happy at all. She was looking older and colorless, as though she were carrying the world's troubles on her shoulders. She certainly didn't look her age—sixteen-going-on-seventeen. She had the general appearance of a mature person who'd suffered many hardships. Lexi felt like crying for her friend. Would she ever stop paying for the mistake she'd made?

The two girls walked together down the street, both lost in their own thoughts. Peggy was distant and remote. Her lips were pressed tightly together, her eyes troubled.

Lexi was equally quiet, her mind whirling. She'd never realized before how a single decision, the one Peggy'd made to be intimate with her boyfriend before marriage, could change so many lives—Peggy's, Chad's, their parents', the baby's, and the adoptive parents'. It made Lexi cringe to think of all the times she'd been careless herself in decisions about other things. Seeing what Peggy was going through made Lexi really think.

As they reached school, Lexi touched Peggy's arm. "I hope you have a good day today, Peggy," she murmured softly.

"Thanks, Lexi."

Before Lexi could say any more, Jennifer Golden came bounding up, her hair shiny in the bright sunlight, her eyes sparkling. "Wasn't the game great last night?" she enthused. "Todd was absolutely super. People all over the school are talking about what a good job he did. He really made an impression."

Lexi was startled to see Minda Hannaford coming toward her with a smile on her face.

"I simply have to find Todd today!" Minda announced when she neared the girls. "He was so awesome on the field last night!" She clapped her hands delightedly. "Next weekend at the Homecoming game, we're going to cream those guys. Everybody thought Todd would be all right, but no one expected him to be this great!"

"Is this weekend Homecoming already?" Peggy gasped.

"Yeah, it's early this year. Isn't that sick? We'll hardly have time to get ready for it. But it doesn't matter as long as we have a good game. And now with Todd as quarterback, we're bound to." Minda's eyes danced. "Of course I've been planning for Homecoming since last summer. I already have my dress. Oh, there's Todd. I've got to go tell him how great he was. Bye! See you later." Minda tripped off happily.

"Why should I get a dress for Homecoming?" Jennifer shrugged. "I'm not taking part in any of the activities."

"Oh, don't pay any attention to Minda," Lexi said with a laugh. "She's happier today than I've seen her in weeks. I think I'll sew myself a new outfit for the big game."

Jennifer turned to Peggy. "You'll be going, won't you Peggy?"

Peggy blinked twice as though she were startled. "What? Huh? Oh, the game. Sure, I suppose."

A wave of sympathy washed over Lexi. It was as though Peggy's life had been taken away from her. She couldn't even be happy about the normal things her friends enjoyed.

At noon, as Lexi was putting away her books and preparing to go to the cafeteria, she saw Chad Allen digging carelessly through his locker. He pulled out a notebook and stuffed it under his arm, shut the door and leaned heavily against it, staring at the floor.

"Chad? Are you all right?" Lexi asked, moving closer to him.

Chad looked as if he were about to slump to the floor in a heap. He lifted his eyes wearily to meet Lexi's. "Huh?" he said blankly.

"Are you feeling all right? Do you want me to get the school nurse?"

Chad shook his head. "Nah. I'm all right. Thanks anyway." His eyes looked glazed. His movements were mechanical and lethargic. The only person Lexi had ever seen behave this way was her grandmother who had Alzheimer's disease.

"Are you going to lunch, Chad?" Lexi inquired.

"No, I don't think so. I'm not very hungry."

Lexi'd never seen anyone so young look so depressed and lifeless.

Just behind Chad, Tim Anders opened his locker door and a stack of books fell out. The loud crash made Lexi jump. Chad didn't even wince.

He's certainly become a loner, Lexi mused as she made her way to the lunchroom. She couldn't remember the last time she'd seen Chad with any of the guys. The way he was acting he wasn't a very appealing friend.

Lexi picked up her tray and went through the cafeteria line. Nothing looked good but a hamburger and a glass of apple juice. Her friends were waiting for her at a table nearby.

Binky was bouncing up and down on the bench like a rubber ball. "Oh, I'm so excited, I can't stand it," she squealed. The table shook. "I've got wonderful news."

"You won a million-dollar sweepstakes," Todd guessed.

"We have a long-lost uncle and he's decided to give us a thousand dollars a month for the rest of our lives," Egg mocked.

"Your mother said you never had to clean your room again," Jennifer put in.

"None of those things. It's more wonderful."

"More wonderful?" Todd echoed. He whistled through his teeth. "This I've got to hear."

"Harry Cramer is coming for Homecoming weekend!"

"That's more wonderful than winning a million dollars? Or never having to clean your room again? Binky, where are your priorities?" Egg asked.

She gave her brother a pained look. "Money isn't everything, you know. I haven't seen Harry in simply ages."

"Oh boy. Now she's going to be walking around the house all goo-goo eyed and dopey. 'Oh, Harry, he's *so* special,' " Egg mimicked.

"Is that really how you act?" Todd turned to Binky. "I can't believe it."

"Quit it! Both of you!" Binky glowered.

"How can you even think about such a shallow subject when *the big game* is coming up?" Egg wondered. "Do you realize it's been years since Cedar River has beaten the Milltown Lions? This is our best chance to stomp all over them—and all you can talk about is boys."

"One boy. Harry Cramer. Now lay off, Egg."

Just then Matt Windsor sauntered up and plunked his lunch tray at the end of the table. "Hey, Todd. Good game last night. What do you think the odds are of winning this weekend?"

Immediately Todd, Egg and Matt launched into a conversation about the Homecoming opponent and the workable plays that might capture a victory. Binky rolled her eyes dramatically. "Men," she mouthed.

Lexi was startled when Todd brought his fist down on the top of the table, making the silverware dance. "This is the year it's going to happen, guys! This is the year we're going to win. We'll beat Milltown no matter what it takes! I've made up my mind."

"Well, you're the quarterback." Egg's eyes gleamed with anticipation. "You're the man who can make it happen."

The whole student body was consumed with football talk, and by Friday Lexi and her friends were getting pretty tired of pep rallies and signs appearing on every locker: Crunch 'em—Smash 'em—Mash Milltown—Lick the Lions.

"Can I hide at your house?" Binky asked Lexi on Friday afternoon. "If I hear one more word about the football game tomorrow, I think I'm going to throw up."

"That bad, huh?"

"I can't stand it anymore. Egg and Todd are constantly talking about plays and strategies and I don't know what else."

"Sure, come on over. We can talk about other things. I'm so excited about the coronation tomorrow afternoon, but I don't dare even mention it to Todd. He thinks that part of Homecoming is frivolous. The most important thing about Homecoming in his eyes is the *big game*, of course."

"He'll think more of the crowning of Homecoming Queen next year," Binky pointed out. "He's not so interested now, because all the candidates are senior girls. Next year, when *we're* seniors, I bet he'll take an interest."

————

Saturday afternoon as Lexi made her way to the gymnasium, she was surprised to see the number of people milling about. She hadn't realized what an active part the community took in the Homecoming festivities. Last year she'd been too new in town to notice.

The gymnasium was decorated with banners and streamers. Large armchairs were placed across the stage for the royalty. The bleachers and the additional chairs on the floor were nearly filled. Fortunately, because the Emerald Tones were singing for the coronation, Lexi didn't have to worry about finding a seat.

Jennifer leaned over to whisper in Lexi's ear as she joined her on the risers. "Can you believe how packed this place is?"

"There's certainly a lot of pomp and circumstance."

"Whatever that means." Jennifer looked puzzled.

Todd, who was standing behind them on the risers, leaned over. "Just let me out of here and at that football game!"

Jennifer gave Todd a quick smile. "I'll bet Lexi will be the Homecoming Queen next year."

Lexi made a face. "Fat chance of that."

"You'd make a beautiful one," Todd agreed.

Lexi laughed, pleased at the compliment. Just then, Mrs. Waverly tapped on the music stand and the band director below the stage raised his arms, the cue for the players to ready their instruments. Everyone stiffened to attention.

Lexi suppressed the smile she felt bubbling within her. Life really was wonderful, especially with friends like hers.

The band played enthusiastically and the Emerald Tones sang with gusto as the royal court marched onto the stage. Though Lexi didn't know any of the candidates well, she was content to watch the proceedings and enjoy the ceremony. She glanced around the jam-packed gymnasium. Everyone in Cedar River seemed to be at the school this afternoon.

Better yet, everyone seemed to be having a wonderful time.

Everyone, that is, except Chad Allen. He sat alone at the far end of the bleachers leaning disconsolately against the painted block wall. His shoulders were slumped and his head bowed. He'd intentionally chosen the one spot where people couldn't crowd around him, and his expression said, "Stay away!"

Lexi turned slightly, leaning toward Todd. "Look at Chad," she whispered.

"I know. I saw him. He looks bad, doesn't he?" Todd glanced around. "Frankly Lexi, I'm really worried about Chad. I can hardly get him to talk to me anymore."

"He's shutting everyone out?"

"There are doors all around him and he's shut and locked them all from the inside."

In the hallway after the coronation, Lexi and Jennifer met Peggy leaning against a wall, trying to avoid the stream of people flowing out the gymnasium doors. "Let's go to the game together tonight," Jennifer suggested.

"Sounds good to me," Lexi agreed. "Can you come, Peggy?"

Peggy nodded absently.

"We'll meet Binky and Harry there."

"Great. We'll all sit in one section so we can really scream and yell. Todd needs his own personal cheering section for this big night."

"Something about this football season must be catchy," Lexi admitted. "I'm getting excited about the game."

Jennifer snorted in a very unladylike manner. "You're just excited to watch Todd play football."

Lexi couldn't deny that. Knowing this was Todd's special night made it exciting for her as well.

As Lexi walked home, she felt like dancing along the sidewalk. *Life is so good,* she thought to herself. She had great friends and a wonderful family. God had given her so much. Lexi was whistling as she entered the back door of her home.

"What are you so cheerful about?" Lexi's mother greeted her. "You sound like a song bird."

Lexi flung herself into a chair and reached for the pitcher of lemonade sitting on the table. "I'm just excited about the game tonight, Mom. This is a real showdown between Cedar River and Milltown. We haven't beaten them in five years, but tonight is going to be the night. Todd is determined to play his best. I'm positive Cedar River will win."

"Well, I hope the game isn't too rough. I'd hate to see Todd get hurt," Mrs. Leighton commented with concern.

"Oh, Mother," Lexi blurted. She couldn't help being a little perturbed with her mom. "Don't be such a worry wart. Todd's a great player and this is going to be a stupendous game."

———

"Do you think this color lipstick looks all right with my sweater?" Binky asked tentatively, obviously nervous about seeing Harry again.

"You look great," said Lexi, encouraging her self-conscious friend.

Jennifer glanced over at Binky's frosted-pink lips. "Hey, what's the deal anyway? You never wear lipstick."

"I am tonight."

"Does Harry like you to wear lipstick?" Jennifer asked, teasing.

"I just want to look nice, that's all." Binky's cheeks flushed a brighter pink than her lips. "If Harry thinks I look nice, so much the better."

The night was crisp and clear, and it was already getting dark. The Homecoming game was scheduled to begin later than usual games. The field was so brightly lit Lexi felt like she needed sunglasses. Suddenly Jennifer pulled a pair out of her shirt pocket and put them on. Lexi covered her mouth to suppress a giggle.

"Lexi, look at Egg," Binky whispered, pointing toward her brother on the sidelines. Egg was flapping around like a windsock in a hurricane. "He's been goofy all day, waiting for this game. Of course, Egg's goofy most of the time. I guess I should be glad there's a reason for it."

Todd and the rest of the team were doing their warm-up exercises in the middle of the field. In their equipment and uniforms they looked big, burly and mean.

Flags reflecting the school colors were flying from the bleachers. Tanya Flanigan, the newly crowned Homecoming Queen, was sitting with her escort in a convertible at the far end of the field. She smiled widely and waved for her fans and their cameras.

Lexi turned her attention to the music as the band began to play a rousing rendition of the school song and then the national anthem. A chill of excitement ran through her. The sound of *The Star-Spangled Banner* always made her think of the beautiful red, white and blue American flag snapping in the wind, of proud soldiers at attention, and of all the wonderful things this free country had given her. Lexi blinked back tears. She didn't want to look silly in front of her friends, but she couldn't help feeling proud and patriotic.

After the band finished, Lexi stood up to watch the cheerleaders enthusiastically getting the fans revved up for the big game. Jennifer, who was obviously not interested in the cheerleaders, was leaning over the side of the bleachers, scouting the activity below.

"What's so interesting down there?" Lexi yelled over the din, her voice fading away as she followed Jennifer's stare and saw someone on the edge of the field. It was Chad.

He was leaning lazily on the front fender of a pick-up. He wore the same clothing he'd worn the day before. His hair appeared uncombed. *That's so unlike Chad,* Lexi mused. *He's usually neat and well-dressed.* Chad had lots of money to spend on clothes and he chose them well. Tonight he looked like a different person.

Suddenly Peggy rounded the corner. Awkwardly, Chad stepped toward her. When Peggy darted away, Chad crumpled against the pick-up door as if he'd taken a blow to the stomach. Lexi felt a curious stab of pity for the boy. He seemed so defenseless, so alone.

Jennifer and Lexi gave each other questioning looks, but before either one could speak, a cheer arose from the crowd and the two girls spun around to face the field. They mustn't miss the game!

Chapter Five

Excitement over the game grew to fever-pitch. The cheerleaders outdid themselves with splits, flips and cartwheels. A member of the percussion section beat on his drum every time the Cedar River team made a good play. The Cougar mascot patrolled the front row of fans with enthusiasm, lifting his arms to lead the crowd in a huge roar. Most of the students knew the furry creature to be Tim Anders.

"Whooo, did he get flattened!" Binky shouted as Todd got sacked. "I hope he's all right."

Lexi bit her lip until the pain made her wince.

As the stack of players untangled themselves one by one, Lexi held her breath. Todd was at the bottom of the pile-up. For what seemed a long time, Todd lay silently on the field while the crowd in the stands held their breath.

Finally, he moved one leg, then the other. Rolling slowly to his side he boosted himself to his feet and a roar went up from the fans.

"Atta boy, Todd!"

"Go get 'em, Winston! You can do it."

The Cougar mascot made a valiant effort at a cartwheel, causing the crowd to relax and laugh as they cheered for Todd.

Binky slumped against Lexi and expelled a relieved sigh. "Todd scared me for a minute. Did you see how long it took him to get up? I was really afraid he was hurt."

Peggy nodded. "For a second I thought he wasn't going to get up. He looked like he was knocked out or something." She put her hand over her heart. "Ooooh, that was scary." Then she gave Lexi a bright smile. "But he won't get hurt, Lexi. He's too tough. Aren't you proud of him?"

Lexi nodded and drew in a steadying breath. Though the air was crisp, she sensed a tang of smoke. Someone was burning leaves—adding to the sights and sounds of fall. It was all so exhilarating. Lexi happily watched Todd trudge across the field to join his teammates.

When Lexi was younger she didn't fully appreciate the scents, sights and sounds around her. Now that she was a little older, she was beginning to value the beautiful world that God had created. She relaxed now. Todd was going to be fine. Everything was great!

The halftime performance included a parade around the football field led by the new Homecoming King and Queen and their royal court. There was special music, and acknowledgement of town dignitaries present. Fireworks culminated the festivities, compliments of the Cedar River Chamber of Commerce.

By the time the second half began, the crowd was worked into a cheerful Homecoming frenzy. Lexi couldn't imagine anyone within a quarter mile of the football field not being excited about the game. Then, unexpectedly, Lexi caught sight of Chad Allen again as he skulked around next to the bleachers. He was standing near a concession stand, one shoulder propped against the booth, his arms crossed belligerently over his chest. Lexi was sure she'd never seen anyone look so gloomy or depressed.

Lexi glanced at Peggy who was intently watching the action on the field, then abruptly stood up. "I have to go to the restroom," Peggy announced. "Does anyone want to come with me?"

"Do you want someone to hold your hand?" Binky teased.

Peggy poked her in the shoulder. "I was just being polite."

"Egg says girls never go to the restroom alone. Only in groups," Binky commented.

"Well, I guess I'll have to show Egg I can manage by myself," Peggy said with a grin. "I'll be right back."

Before Lexi could reach out to stop her, Peggy was gone. To reach the restrooms, she had to pass directly by the concession stand where Chad waited. From Lexi's perch on top of the bleachers, she had a bird's eye view.

When Chad saw Peggy coming, he faded into the shadows. When she was inches from him he stepped out, caught her by the arm and pulled her toward him. Lexi saw Peggy stiffen and struggle to get away. But Chad wouldn't let go. He leaned closer, thrust his face at hers, and spoke rapidly.

Peggy shook her head defiantly.

Lexi unconsciously gripped the edge of the railing until her knuckles were white. *What are Peggy and*

*Chad talking about? What is he saying to her? Why
can't he just leave her alone? When will he understand?* Lexi's thoughts raced as she stared at the
scene unfolding below. Peggy raised her hand and
soundly slapped Chad's cheek. Even at a distance,
Lexi could see Chad's stunned expression. When he
dropped Peggy's arm, she darted into the women's
restroom.

Chad waited outside the door a moment, then
slipped away into the darkness. After a few minutes,
Lexi looked again to see the restroom door open and
Peggy peek outside to confirm that Chad had gone.

Binky whispered to Lexi, "Wake up! The game is
almost over!"

Reluctantly Lexi tore her gaze from Peggy and
faced the field again. Lexi watched with guarded interest as the Cedar River Cougars trounced the Milltown Lions soundly and the game ended with a
standing ovation from the fans.

The cheerleaders presented the annual Homecoming awards for the most enthusiastic cheer-
leader, the most patient classroom advisor, and a host
of other nonsensical awards that everyone except
Lexi seemed to enjoy.

After the awards the pep band played a final song,
and Lexi scrambled to look for Peggy. But she was
nowhere to be seen.

Lexi searched for another ten minutes, and then
Tressa Williams came sauntering up to her, snapping her gum.

"Hey, Leighton, I've got a message for you."

"For me?"

"Yeah. From Peggy Madison. She was tearing out

of here like a monster was after her, and told me to tell you that she was going home. She said she was sorry she couldn't stay, but she'd call you tomorrow. Got it?"

"Thanks Tressa." Lexi's mind whirled with what had gone on between Chad and Peggy. She couldn't shake her thoughts when Binky caught up to her.

"Harry and I are going out for a while. Do you and Todd want to come with us?"

Lexi shook her head distractedly. "No. I don't think so. I'll just wait here for him. You go ahead."

"Are you sure?"

"I know you two want to be alone." Lexi smiled at Binky. "You haven't had a chance to talk for a long time."

Binky blushed a little. "Well, that's true. But you're always welcome, you know."

"I know, Bink. Thanks anyway. Maybe another time."

Binky disappeared into the crowd and Lexi moved closer to the locker room door. She sat down on a stool, leaned her head against the cold block wall and closed her eyes. Normally it would have been the football game replaying in her mind, but the only image that flashed before her was that of Peggy and Chad fighting in the dim light of the concession stand.

"Wow! What a game!" Some boys walked by Lexi, chortling about the victory. "That Winston is going to be some quarterback!"

"What do you mean, going to be? He already is!"

"If he doesn't lose his cool on the field."

"I can see it now. This is going to be one of Cedar

River's greatest years ever."

The voices faded and Lexi closed her eyes again, wishing she could will away the ugly scene that kept repeating itself in her mind.

"Lexi. Are you okay?" Todd's soft voice broke into her painful reverie.

"Oh, Todd! I'm glad you're ready. It was, uh—a great game. Congratulations!

"Is something wrong?"

Todd looked so wonderful to Lexi. His golden hair was darker when it was wet. "You didn't dry off very well," Lexi pointed out with a smile.

"I knew you were waiting outside." Todd shook his head and Lexi felt droplets of water spray across her face. "It's a nice night. I'll air-dry while we're walking. Do you want to go to the Hamburger Shack or the Homecoming reception?"

Lexi hesitated. There were lots of Homecoming activities going on. Until an hour ago, she would have been happy to take part in any of them. But now the image of Peggy and Chad was burned into her mind and she knew she couldn't enjoy anything that was the least bit lighthearted.

"I don't think I'm in the mood, Todd."

His brow furrowed. "Not in the mood? We won the game! Something's wrong, Lexi. You'd better tell me what it is."

She blurted out the scenario at the concession stand. "I don't know what's going on between them, Todd, but Chad disappeared and Peggy ran home without speaking to me. Something is radically wrong. I just know it. I can feel it."

"I've been feeling it too, but I really don't know

what to do about it." Todd swung his duffle bag across his shoulder and reached for Lexi's hand. "Come on."

They walked in companionable silence for a long time. Finally Todd tipped his head backward and stared up at the stars. He sighed deeply. "I've been thinking about Chad a lot lately, wondering what went wrong with him."

"What do you think did?"

"I don't know. I've been thinking about his family, though. They're quite wealthy. His father owns a large manufacturing plant on the edge of town and he's grooming his son for the family business. Chad doesn't really have a choice in the matter. His father's planned his life for him. After high school he has to go to college and get an MBA. Then his dad expects him to return to Cedar River to take over the plant."

Lexi supposed the Allens felt a responsibility to the community as one of the early settlers in Cedar River. They were one of the first families to invest in the unpopulated area. Chad hinted on occasion that his family cared more about protecting the family name than any one individual member.

"I think there's something wrong with the way Chad's family operates," Todd said, echoing Lexi's silent thoughts. "Chad always has plenty of money and lots of material things, but I think his parents really expect a lot from him in return. It seems like Chad's dad sets him up to feel like a failure no matter what he accomplishes or how much effort he puts into it. Mr. Allen expects Chad to be perfect, and there's no way any kid can live up to that. Chad used to talk to me about it a lot before he started dating Peggy."

"Can't Chad tell his dad how he feels?"

"Chad—talk to his dad?" Todd chuckled. "He'd have to make an appointment! Chad told me once that his dad never comes home from the office before nine or ten at night. And he's always gone again when Chad gets up in the morning. When are you supposed to talk to a man like that?"

"Poor Chad," Lexi murmured. Although she was angry with him for the way he treated Peggy, she did feel compassion for the boy. He seemed so miserable.

"I've been keeping an eye on Chad for quite a while now," Todd continued. "A lot of things have changed for him since Peggy got pregnant. For a long time he's seemed down . . . just—"

"Depressed?" Lexi asked.

"You could call it that. Very unhappy. I figured it was natural, that he was probably feeling guilty about Peggy. Then he began to get worse."

"Worse? How?"

"There's a hopelessness about him. He acts as if nothing matters. Like there's nothing he cares about. Do you remember the last time you actually saw Chad smile?"

Lexi honestly couldn't remember. "No. Of course, I haven't seen him as much as you."

"Well, that's the other thing. He doesn't want to be around people anymore. He'd rather be alone. It's like he's observing life instead of living it. He talked to me about it once."

"What did he say?"

"He was kind of weird about the whole thing. He talked about Peggy's pregnancy and how he supposed she'd never want to speak to him again. Then he made this crazy switch and he started talking about the two of them starting over. He wanted everything to be like it was before. It's as though his mind is stuck in a rut. He keeps going over the same things again and again. I can't get him to talk about anything else. I've never seen anyone so unhappy in my whole life, Lexi. And worse yet, he doesn't seem to know how to do anything about it."

"I didn't realize," Lexi said softly. "I've been feeling angry with Chad because I've heard Peggy's side of the story."

"Peggy has suffered plenty, but Chad's been suffering too. I don't know what to do for him anymore. When he chooses to isolate himself from everyone, there's not much anyone can do."

"Could we think of a way for Chad to spend time with us?" Lexi asked. "He's proud of being a good student. Maybe you two could study together."

"He *was* a good student. Not anymore. I overheard one of the teachers threaten him with a failing grade if he didn't shape up in class."

"Chad? I can't believe that. The school year's hardly started."

"I know, but he hasn't been turning in any papers. Chad doesn't seem to be interested in any of the things he used to love."

Lexi was puzzled. She didn't fully understand what was going on. "Chad wouldn't try to hurt himself, would he?" she blurted. The thought made her shudder.

Instead of giving her a comforting no for an answer, Todd shrugged his shoulders. "I don't know. He told me once when he was really down that he wasn't sure life was worth living anymore. I gave him a big pep-talk about how that wasn't true. I told him that he should go talk to the school counselor."

"Did he?"

"He said he would, but I don't know if he ever did."

"His parents were supposed to arrange for some counseling," Lexi said. "But I never heard any more about it. I suppose they wanted to keep that confidential."

"I hope they force him to go. I don't like the way Chad's been talking lately. I hate hearing him say he's worthless or that he's a big burden to everyone around him."

"Chad's a talented guy who got himself into a big mess and now he can't seem to find his way out," Lexi repeated woodenly.

Todd turned to Lexi and looked at her squarely. "It could have been us, Lexi. We're no better than Chad and Peggy. We've just made some different choices."

Lexi nodded silently. She would always be thankful that she and Todd had decided long ago to save themselves for marriage. If Chad had made that decision, the problems he faced now would not exist.

"Here we are," Todd said finally as they neared the Leighton house. "Looks dark. Everyone must be in bed."

"Dad said he was going to bed early tonight. He was pretty tired. He did surgery at the veterinary clinic today. Would you like to come inside?"

Todd hesitated, then shook his head. "I don't think so. I'm tired too. It was a big game."

"And you were wonderful, Todd. I'm sorry I was so distracted by everything else." The admiration in Lexi's voice was enough.

"It was fun. We have a good team this year."

"You mean we have a good *quarterback* this year," Lexi corrected.

Todd leaned down and kissed her softly. "At least the quarterback has a good cheering section," he said, smiling. "Good night, Lexi. See you tomorrow."

Chapter Six

Lexi had been sleeping soundly. Her arms and legs felt like two-ton weights. Then her mother's hand was on her arm and Lexi moaned, "I'm sleeping in today."

Somehow she knew that her mother had chosen to ignore the comment. Lexi buried her face in her pillow. "Just another half hour, Mom. I don't want to get up now. I need to sleep." The shades on her windows snapped up and the bright sunlight streamed in. "Mom! Give me ten minutes. I was having the most wonderful dream . . ."

"Lexi, I'd like you to get up."

"Ten more minutes? In my dream I was on a beautiful beach with miles and miles of ocean. Egg was the lifeguard . . ."

"Lexi, please, I need to talk to you."

The tone of Mrs. Leighton's voice told Lexi her mother was not going to change her mind.

"Mom? Is something wrong?" Lexi forced herself into a sitting position.

Her mother sat down on the far end of the bed and folded her hands in her lap. "We need to talk, Lexi."

Lexi felt a tickling sensation of fear in the pit of her stomach. The last time her mother had behaved like this was when she'd told her that Grandfather Carson was ill. Now Lexi was wide awake. "Mom, what's happened? Is everything okay? Dad? Ben?"

"Dad and Ben are fine, Lexi. But we've had some very shocking news."

"What kind of news?" Lexi's stomach lurched like she'd come out of the biggest dip in a roller coaster ride.

"Chad Allen committed suicide last night."

Lexi felt like she'd been hit with a sack of bricks. She gasped sharply, and the tears came abruptly. "No! It can't be. It just can't be! I saw Chad last night at the football game." The image of Chad looking dirty, rumpled and forlorn flashed into Lexi's mind. "He didn't look good—but he was alive."

"I'm so sorry, Lexi. We got the phone call about half an hour ago."

"He couldn't have committed suicide, Mom. It can't be true. It must be a mistake. An accident— somebody else . . ."

"I'm sorry, Lexi, but it *was* Chad."

"No!" The wail tore at her throat. Lexi launched herself into her mother's arms, sobbing. Mrs. Leighton held her tightly, rocking her and consoling her as best she could.

"It's all right, Lexi. We'll get through this. We'll handle it with God's help."

"But what about Chad's parents? And . . ." Lexi drew a sharp gasp, "what about *Peggy*, Mom?"

"Don't think about it now, Lexi."

But she shivered uncontrollably, as though her

body had gone berserk. Waves of hot and cold washed through her. "Chad . . . Poor Chad," she sobbed.

Mrs. Leighton pulled the comforter from the end of the bed and wrapped it around her daughter. After several minutes, Lexi managed to sit up. "How did it happen, Mom?"

"All the details aren't in yet, Lexi. I'm not sure you'll want to . . ."

"I want to know, Mom. I have to know."

Mrs. Leighton sighed. "I don't want to upset you anymore, Lexi."

"I'll be upset if I don't know. He was my classmate, Mom. He was my friend."

"No one knows everything yet, Lexi. But Chad must have had an argument last night—words with Peggy that upset him very much."

The image of the two in the pale light of the concession stand flooded Lexi's mind again.

"Anyway, Chad left the football field and went to the Convention Center where a band was warming up for a concert."

"Several of my friends talked about going to that concert last night," Lexi said.

"Well, Chad met someone at the Convention Center who gave him some pills."

"Pills?" Lexi said weakly.

"From there he went to the Hamburger Shack where he met several friends from school. They said he was acting very strangely—talking loudly and laughing."

"Laughing? Chad hasn't laughed in weeks."

"He was bragging about the pills he had. He even took them out and showed them to the boys. He told them he was going to go home and take them—along with some his mother had in her medicine cabinet."

Lexi's jaw dropped in astonishment. "They knew? And they didn't try to stop him?"

"They didn't take him seriously, Lexi. They couldn't believe someone contemplating suicide would hang out at the Hamburger Shack showing off pills and telling everyone what he was going to do."

"No, I suppose not. It doesn't make sense to me, either."

"It was a cry for help, Lexi. Chad wanted someone to stop him, but no one did."

The sadness of the situation overwhelmed Lexi as her mother continued: "Then Chad called Peggy in the middle of the night and spoke incoherently."

"Did he tell Peggy he was going to kill himself?" Lexi wondered. The story was becoming more horrible by the minute.

"Apparently. He told Peggy that if she didn't come back to him and have the same relationship they'd had before, he would end his life."

"Oh, Chad. What a stupid thing to do! And poor Peggy!"

"She wouldn't be manipulated, and called her father. Mr. Madison tried to talk to Chad, but he became very agitated. He must have realized that Peggy wasn't going to give in or change her mind, so he hung up. When Peggy tried to call him back, the line was busy. Chad had taken the phone off the hook."

"That's when he did it? When he took the pills?"

"Apparently he'd already taken them when he made the call. Mr. Madison called the police but it was too late."

A weak wail escaped Lexi's lips and she sank limply against her mother. "This is so awful I can't believe it. I can't understand it. I should have done something."

"You, Lexi? What could you have done?"

"Something. Anything. I saw Chad last night. I didn't talk to him. I didn't tell him that I cared about him. I . . ."

"It's common to feel guilty after a suicide, Lexi, but there was nothing you could have done. This was Chad's choice and Chad's action."

"I should have told him that he meant something to me. That I forgave him for his behavior with Peggy. That . . ."

Mrs. Leighton stroked her daughter's back. "Don't Lexi. Don't blame yourself for this. Chad is gone. 'What if's' will only bring you more pain. We can learn from this for the future, but we can't go back, Lexi."

"I just don't understand, Mom. Even though Peggy wouldn't go out with him anymore, there are lots of girls that would have dated Chad Allen, if he'd asked them."

"Maybe, Lexi. The facts don't support his action. Chad was a handsome, talented boy. But deep inside he must not have known or believed it.

"Sometimes people sink so low into depression and self-pity that they begin to think their situation is permanent—that there's no way out. Death is the only solution they can see." Mrs. Leighton rubbed Lexi's back as she spoke.

"Teenage boys and girls break up every day. But for some reason, the rejection was too much for Chad.

He lost his self-worth and couldn't face another day."

"But that's stupid!" Lexi felt angry with Chad. "Another day would have been better—brighter. I could have told him that."

"Of course you could have, Lexi, but he may not have believed you. It's my guess that Chad was suffering feelings of extreme rejection and a sense of failure with the loss of an important friendship."

"You mean it was Peggy's fault?"

"Not at all, Lexi." Mrs. Leighton shook her head. "Not at all. Chad was a troubled boy. I think he had problems at home, at school, everywhere. He needed help and didn't get it fast enough. It's difficult to say what tipped Chad over the edge into despair. I'm sure it wasn't any one single thing—nothing that any of you could blame yourself for.

"It's like the old adage, 'It was the straw that broke the camel's back.' One straw wouldn't be felt, but a straw added to hundreds of pounds of straw could be the one that breaks a camel's back."

"Chad wanted Peggy to make him first in her life. When she couldn't, he refused to go on living," Lexi tried to reason what had happened.

"And that was Chad's choice, Lexi. Not Peggy's. Not yours. It was a wrong choice, a bad choice, but no one took those pills for him. He did it himself."

Lexi was silent for a long time. Her mind whirled with the shocking news. *Chad is gone. But where?* "Mom, does it talk about suicide in the Bible?"

Mrs. Leighton held Lexi a little closer. "Yes it does, honey. Suicide has been common as long as history has been recorded. Ironically, the verses in the Bible that refer to it reveal that men killed themselves for pretty insignificant reasons. None seemed good or wise."

"Like what, Mom?"

"Well, in First Samuel, Saul killed himself by falling on his own sword after a defeat in battle. I suppose he was so discouraged and humiliated he no longer wanted to live. Saul's faithful armor-bearer did the same thing, imitating the death of his master. And Samson, in the book of Judges, pulled the Philistine temple down to kill his enemies, dying with them in the process."

Mrs. Leighton contemplated what she knew of Bible accounts. "There really aren't many stories about suicides in the Bible. Those who believed in God considered themselves the Lord's property. The only suicide I know of in the New Testament was Judas' after he betrayed Jesus."

"But doesn't the Bible say anything about suicide itself?"

"There are scriptures that certainly discourage it, like Matthew 10:22: 'He who endures to the end will be saved.' As long as a man lives and breathes, he has the opportunity to repent and turn to God, but if a man takes his own life, that opportunity is gone. And, of course, suicide is murder—and the Bible expressly forbids that."

"This is so complicated!" Lexi felt panic welling up within her.

"No, Lexi. It's not complicated. God is the only one who has the right to give life or to take it away. Suicide takes that right from God."

"But what will happen to Chad? Where is he now?"

"He's in God's hands, Lexi, and He will do what is right. That's all we know. It's up to God. We can't second-guess Him."

"But isn't there anything we can do?"

"As cold and callous as this might seem, Lexi, all we can do is go on with our lives. We're going to have to pull ourselves together so that we can be strong for Chad's family and for Peggy. That's all we can do."

"I don't think I can, Mom. I can't be strong for anyone."

Mrs. Leighton rubbed her daughter's shoulder. "It seems difficult, but like everything else in life, you have to take things one step at a time. Why don't you take a shower and get dressed, and I'll go downstairs and make you some breakfast."

"I couldn't eat, Mom. Not now."

"I want you to try. Like I said, we have to be strong for the people who are left."

Lexi swung her feet to the side of the bed and stood up. She felt as weak as a kitten.

Mrs. Leighton reached for Lexi's robe. "Here, slip this on. Take your time. I'll have something ready when you come downstairs."

Lexi made her way to the bathroom. The steaming shower did feel good on her back. She imagined that it pummeled away some of her pain, hurt and confusion. It washed away the tears that continued to fall. After some time there was a tap on the door. "Who is it?" she called.

"Are you drowning, Lexi?" Ben's voice was small and worried. "I'm scared. You don't come out."

"Sorry, Ben. I didn't mean to scare you. The water felt good."

"Mom's got breakfast ready. She says I can't eat until you come down."

"Well, I'd better hurry then, okay, Ben?"

"Ben will go downstairs and wait for you."

While Lexi toweled herself dry, her mind raced in a million directions. *Where was God in all of this?* she wondered. *Why did He let this happen? How could Chad do such a thing? How? Why?* The questions collided with each other in her mind until her head ached.

Lexi chose a pair of khaki-colored slacks and an oversized dark brown top from her closet. She brushed her damp hair away from her face and slowly descended the steps to the kitchen. Dr. and Mrs. Leighton and Ben were waiting for her.

"Mom, there's no way I can eat pancakes today," Lexi protested as she looked at the table.

"Just one. And a slice of bacon. Remember what I said."

Slowly, as though she were a hundred years old, Lexi lowered herself to the chair. She took a tentative bite of the food on her plate. Much to her amazement, it tasted good. She found herself eating one pancake and then another.

"Would you like a third, Lexi?"

Lexi shook her head.

Mrs. Leighton gave her a wry smile. "Life does go on, Lexi. Things like showers and pancakes, and people like your little brother are still here. They're what will get you through the next few weeks with God's help. Remember that. It's the simple yet wonderful gifts from God that make you know you're still a part of this world."

When she was finished with breakfast, Lexi pushed away from the table with a determined thrust. "I have to go to Peggy's," she said, expecting an argument from her parents. There was none.

"We thought you might want to, Lexi. Are you sure you want to go this morning?"

"I have to go. Peggy needs me."

"I'm sure she does. If you think you're up to it, go ahead. Would you like one of us to come along?"

Lexi looked from her mother's face to her father's. "Thank you. I know you'd like to help, but this is something I have to do by myself."

The sun was shining as Lexi walked down the sidewalk to the Madison home. Amazing! Nothing was changed. The houses looked the same. The trees stood tall and unmoved. A dog barked familiarly in the distance. The sun felt warm on her shoulders. How could everything be so normal when her world was turned upside down?

There were several cars in the Madison driveway. For a moment, Lexi almost lost her nerve. Then, with a prayer for strength, she mounted the steps and rang the doorbell. Peggy's mother came to the door. Her eyes were puffy and red. It was obvious she'd been crying.

"Lexi." She reached out and folded her arms around Lexi's shoulders. "I'm so glad you're here. Peggy needs you."

"How is she, Mrs. Madison?" Lexi was amazed at how steady her voice sounded.

"Stunned. Shocked. Devastated. It's as though the full impact of what's happened hasn't quite sunk in yet. She's been walking around the house in a daze. I'm afraid of what state she'll be in when it finally hits her."

"Is there anything I can do?"

"Just be here for her, honey. That's all any of us can do right now. She's going to need some counseling. We all are. Today, all you can do is let her know that you love her."

The living room was full of people. Some were strangers to Lexi. Some she recognized as relatives of the Madisons. They were all quiet and somber. Peggy was nowhere to be seen.

Suddenly she appeared in the doorway. "Lexi, there you are. I've been waiting for you." Her voice was flat and lifeless. There were no tears and she didn't seem agitated. "You've heard?"

Lexi nodded.

"It isn't true, Lexi. It can't be. I know it isn't true. Chad would never do a thing like that . . ."

With her arms open, Peggy ran to Lexi and hugged her tightly, then began to weep in deep heaving sobs. Lexi had never felt so helpless in her entire life.

Chapter Seven

It was late afternoon when Lexi finally returned home. She walked slowly, feeling numb. The day had taken on a nightmarish quality that frightened her. Memories of Chad consumed her thoughts. In trying to keep Peggy together, Lexi felt herself coming unglued.

Peggy alternated between calm reasoning to outspoken denial that Chad was really gone. First she spoke in long rambling sentences about Chad and the things they'd done together, then lapsed into periods of mournful silence that frightened Lexi even more. She felt as if she'd ridden an emotional roller coaster all day long and was exhausted.

It was difficult to believe that Chad was gone *forever*. Forever was a strange word. How could a person even begin to imagine the idea of no longer existing? Never to return.

Lexi knew in her heart that Chad hadn't imagined being gone forever, either. If he had, he never would have done this terrible thing. She was sure that his taking the pills was an impulsive, desperate move. He hadn't thought this out clearly. Chad had tried to punish Peggy for rejecting him, never realizing what a permanent act he was committing. A foolish, impulsive, permanent act. Forever and ever. The end.

When Lexi reached her house, she was surprised to see Todd, Egg, Binky, and Jennifer all sitting on the porch steps. Their faces were masks of pain.

"Lexi," Todd murmured, and opened his arms. She ran into them.

Soon all five were hugging and holding one another, weeping together on the front steps. Lexi wiped away her tears with a fist. "Maybe we should go inside. People driving by will think we've lost our minds at this house."

"Mine's been gone quite awhile," Egg made a feeble attempt at humor. "But I suppose you should consider your own reputation."

They made their way to the living room where Dr. and Mrs. Leighton were sitting. "Come on in, kids. Sit down." Lexi's parents looked somber. "Do you mind if a couple *old* folks join you? We're feeling a little blue ourselves right now."

"We'd like to have you stay," Todd said politely. "Maybe you can help us understand what's happened. I know I can't figure it out on my own."

"Why did he do it? That's what I want to know," Egg blurted. "Chad wasn't crazy. How could anyone in his right mind decide to kill himself?" Egg's flushed face showed his anger.

"It was a senseless, impulsive move. That's all I can figure out," Todd said, echoing Lexi's earlier thoughts.

"Once dead, always dead," Binky said indignantly. "He should have known that. Dead means *gone*, never coming back." She, too, was angry at the thought of a classmate so rudely jerked away from life.

Jennifer was silent, her chin propped on the heels of her hands. Her eyes were narrowed in thought. Instinctively, Lexi knew that Jennifer was about to ask a question.

"Does anyone know what really happened?"

Lexi weighed her words carefully before responding. She told them what she had seen at the football game—about Chad grabbing Peggy and Peggy slapping him across the face. "He wouldn't leave her alone," Lexi explained. "That was what Peggy kept repeating, even today. She kept saying, 'He wouldn't leave me alone.' He wouldn't believe that it was over. He was obsessed with it. With her."

"I don't get it," Binky said. "Guys and girls break up all the time. That doesn't mean you have to kill yourself. If Harry and I broke up tomorrow, I'd be hurt and I'd cry. I'd probably think it was the worst thing that ever happened to me, but I wouldn't kill myself."

"That's because you're balanced emotionally, Binky," Mrs. Leighton responded. "Something snapped in Chad. Something made him think that he couldn't live without the relationship he'd had with Peggy."

"Chad wasn't close to his parents," Todd interjected. "Maybe he thought he'd lost the last person in the world who cared about him."

Egg cleared his throat. His Adam's apple bounced up and down and a deep blush spread across his face. "What's wrong, Egg?" Todd asked.

"I . . . uh . . . oh well, never mind."

"Spit it out, Egg," Binky said. "You've got a question."

"It's a question I shouldn't be asking. It's just—it just keeps coming to my mind."

"What is it?" Dr. Leighton asked.

"How? How did he do it?" He dropped his eyes to his hands, which were wringing awkwardly in his lap. "That's a gruesome question, I know, but for some reason, I'm curious."

Dr. Leighton cleared his throat and everyone's attention turned to him. "It's a valid question, Egg. Don't be ashamed of honest questions. It's normal to wonder. I'll explain what I know. But I want you all to promise me that you won't dwell on this. Think of Chad as the good friend that he was, not the troubled boy that he'd become in the last few weeks."

The conversation continued for a long time. It was obvious that everyone needed the closeness, support, and reassurance they could receive from close friends and family in the Leighton living room. It was also comforting to know that the world was progressing despite this hideous thing that had happened.

Ben came in from the yard, carrying his bunny. "I'm taming Bunny. Does anyone want to pet him?" Ben inquired innocently.

The contrast between the gloom and sadness the young people were feeling and Ben's cheerful face was startling.

"I'll pet the bunny," Jennifer offered.

"Would you like to feed him a carrot?" Ben asked eagerly. "I have one in my pocket." He pulled a carrot, fresh from the garden—chunks of dirt and all—

out of the rear pocket of his jeans.

"Oh, Benjamin! It's all dirty, honey."

"Bunny loves carrots," Ben explained.

"Better get the hand vacuum, Lexi, before we track dirt all over the house," Mrs. Leighton said.

Ben's innocent entrance had shattered the mournful mood. Everyone began to laugh and talk of other things.

Mrs. Leighton stood up. "It's almost suppertime. We're having pizza. Is anyone interested in staying?"

"Sure!" "Yeah!" "Count me in!" chorused from the hungry group.

"Better call your mothers and let them know where you are. Then if you'll wash your hands, you can all help me make the pizza."

Todd took charge of rolling out the dough. Jennifer grated cheese, and Egg sliced the pepperoni. Binky worked on the sauce with Mrs. Leighton, while Lexi and her father made lemonade and set the table.

Ben soon joined them, demanding brownies for dessert. Mrs. Leighton gave him a packaged mix and a bowl and told him he could make them himself. Ben hummed cheerfully, asking a million questions as he stirred up the batter.

When Ben started to sing "Row, Row, Row Your Boat," everyone joined in parts and sang the song in a round. For another hour the group enjoyed food, fellowship and the warmth of one another's company in the safe haven of the Leighton kitchen. At least temporarily, the dark shadows cast on their lives by the death of their friend were dispelled.

Late that evening, after Lexi's friends had gone

home, Mrs. Leighton knocked on her bedroom door. "May I come in?" She peeked through the opening. "You aren't asleep, are you?"

"I don't feel like I'll ever be able to sleep again. My mind won't turn off, Mom. It just keeps spinning with questions."

"Listen, honey, I know I don't have all the answers for you or your friends, but Dad and I just want you to know that we're here for you. We'll do our best to offer any guidance and insight we can. This is a tough time for all of you."

"Thanks, Mom. I really appreciate that. It's just that sometimes there are questions you can't answer."

"What kind of questions, Lexi?"

I've never really thought about suicide before— about how it would feel. Now I've asked myself, would I ever try it? What would make me do something like that? I think about Chad and the pills he took, and why he chose that way. What is it like to feel so low that suicide is your best answer?" Lexi shuddered. "It scares me, Mom. Those questions keep gnawing at my mind like evil little mice."

"You're not alone with your questions, Lexi. You kids have been faced for the first time with the death of a peer. If you asked each of your friends, they'd probably admit to having the same sort of questions. Don't be afraid to voice your thoughts. Get them out in the open. Tell them to someone. Talk about them. You see, that was Chad's mistake. He didn't get support when things started to go wrong for him. Finally he felt so isolated and alone that he thought there was no hope."

"So talking helps then?"

"I think it does," Mrs. Leighton said. "There are a lot of therapists who believe it's the first step to help. We have to be honest with each other, Lexi. And right now is not the time to hide anything—thoughts, feelings or emotions. It's best to get them out in the open where they can be dealt with."

"I just hope Peggy has someone telling her these things, Mom. She's really mixed up right now." Lexi lay back against her pillows. "Poor Peggy. Everything's gone wrong for her this past year."

Mrs. Leighton nodded. "I know. That's why Peggy needs help more than the rest of us. She's had many things to deal with. She needs our support and she needs to talk. Promise me something, Lexi?"

"Sure, Mom, what?"

"If Peggy ever tells you that her life's not worth living, promise that you'll tell someone? Either me or Peggy's mother, or one of your teachers. Let's make sure she gets help right away. I hope she never gets to that point, but right now she's carrying a heavy burden for a young girl."

"Sure, Mom. Of course I'll tell someone." Lexi shivered at the thought that Peggy might want to follow the same path Chad had taken. All this was so complicated and frightening. Still, all that could be done now was to attempt to pull the pieces back together and go on with life.

Chapter Eight

It was going to be the most difficult day of her life. Lexi knew it the moment she opened her eyes. Today was Chad's memorial service.

She'd been to her grandfather's funeral, and it was sad. But Grandfather had lived a long productive life. Lexi had mourned her own loss. It had been difficult to realize that Grandfather would not be there for her when she had questions to ask or concerns to discuss. But despite her tears, Lexi had the assurance that her grandfather was in heaven.

Today's service would be different. Chad had not died at the end of a long, happy life. His had ended abruptly, violently, and much too early. Her grandfather's death was more or less expected, something that came with old age. But Chad's life was just beginning—and now it was over.

Lexi didn't want to get out of bed. If there were any way she could miss this day, she would have. She swallowed hard a couple of times, hoping to feel pain or scratchiness in her throat, some hint that she was not well enough to go. She felt her forehead, hoping to find it feverish. Any excuse would do. Any excuse to avoid the difficulty of facing this day.

"You'd better get up, Lexi." Her mother stepped into the bedroom without knocking. "Everyone else has used the shower. I told Mrs. Winston that we'd meet them outside the church."

"I don't want to go, Mom," Lexi protested. "Do I have to?"

"Of course, Lexi. I know this is terribly difficult for all of you, but it's important that you go. Peggy needs you there, and it's a way to say goodbye to Chad."

"But I don't want to say goodbye!"

"I understand, Lexi, but it has to be done. Turning your back on today won't help or change anything."

With a soft groan, Lexi rolled to the side of her bed and stood up. "What should I wear?"

Mrs. Leighton opened her daughter's closet. "There are several outfits that would do." She pulled out a dark green jumper. "How about this with a white blouse?"

"You mean you don't have to wear black to funerals?" Lexi asked. "I always thought you did."

"Not anymore. You didn't wear black to your grandfather's funeral. I think this will be just fine, Lexi." Mrs. Leighton laid the outfit across the foot of the bed. "Hurry up, now. We can't be late."

Lexi moved slowly through the routine of showering and dressing. "Where's Ben?" she asked when she entered the kitchen.

"He's gone to a friend's house," Mrs. Leighton explained. "I thought it would be best if he didn't attend the funeral."

Lexi was glad for her mother's decision. At least

Ben wouldn't have to go through this.

Dr. Leighton pulled into the driveway just as Lexi finished her breakfast. He walked into the house, shed his white veterinarian coat and reached for the suit jacket draped on the back of a dining room chair. "Ready?"

"Did you close the office, Dad?"

"My secretary's still there. I juggled some appointments."

"I'm glad you're coming, Dad. I'm glad you're both coming."

"We would never let you go through this alone, Lexi," her father said, hugging her gently.

The three got into the family car and were silent for the short drive to the church. The parking lot was full, as well as the streets on all sides. Lexi spotted her classmates scattered through the crowd that milled outside the sanctuary.

"There's Todd and his parents," Mrs. Leighton pointed out. Todd was wearing a dark blue suit. His golden hair was slicked back, giving him a more grown-up look.

"And there's Matt Windsor," Lexi added. "And Anna Marie Arnold. I see Mary Beth Adamson too, and Tim Anders." Lexi glanced around the parking area for familiar faces. "Jennifer. Minda Hannaford. And here come Tressa and Gina Williams."

It was comforting to have her friends and classmates around her.

"Will your friends all sit together, Lexi?" her mother asked.

Lexi shook her head. "No. We decided we'd rather sit with our parents. We thought it might be easier."

Lexi gave a humorless laugh. "As if anything could make this easier."

Todd came to Lexi's side and took her hand, squeezing it tightly. The comforting gesture made Lexi's eyes fill with tears again. She looked at him and choked back the lump in her throat.

"There's Peggy," Todd whispered.

Peggy made her way toward the church, her mother and father supporting her on either side. It appeared Peggy would not have had the strength to walk on her own.

"I feel so badly for her, Todd," Lexi murmured. "She blames herself for Chad's death. She thinks that if she'd given in to Chad, this never would have happened."

Mrs. Winston laid a comforting hand on Lexi's arm. "Peggy's wrong, Lexi. Chad was disturbed. It may take her awhile to realize it, but she's not to blame for this."

Lexi stared at Peggy as she and her parents entered the church. Her heart ached for her friend.

Ever since the news of Chad's death, Lexi felt as though her emotions were raging out of control. Briefly she'd forget what had happened, then it would all come rushing back and she wanted to weep. If she were this devastated, how must Peggy feel?

"I think it's time to go inside," Dr. Leighton spoke to Todd. "Why don't you and Lexi lead the way?"

The bank of flowers at the front of the church was a lush mass of golden fall hues—bronze and coral, yellow and red, orange, russet, and deep green. The sanctuary filled quickly as Lexi followed Todd to the center of the church. They sat with their parents directly in front of Minda and the other High-Fives. The girls were crying softly. Minda's sobs could be heard above the others. The organ music swelled and was soothing to Lexi's jangled emotions. She closed her eyes and soaked in the message of the unspoken words that she knew by heart.

At eleven o'clock sharp Pastor Horace stepped into the pulpit. He looked older than usual, as though burdened by the weight of the job ahead of him.

"This is a very difficult moment in my ministry," he began. "It is a time when one feels being a pastor must be the hardest job in the world.

"As we are gathered here today, questions are no doubt raging in your minds, especially the minds of our young people. 'Why did this happen? What could we have done to prevent it? How can we go ahead with our own lives? How do we deal with the memories? The guilt? The sadness?' " Lexi's attention was already riveted to his words.

"Suicide is an unanswered question. Is it a sin that should be condemned and denounced? Is it an illness, a weakness of mind, heart and spirit for which we should express sympathy and grief? Is it a choice that, once made, we should accept? Perhaps it is all three—a sin, an illness, a choice. After long hours of thought and prayer, I have come to this conclusion: We must put this question and Chad Allen in God's loving, supremely capable hands.

"There are many feelings, many emotions represented here today. Anger. Resentment. Guilt. Sadness. Regret. Each of us feels them to some degree or another. Don't ignore your feelings. Don't suppress them into your subconscious mind. Recognize them. Deal with them.

"The feelings you have today are neither wrong nor right. They are simply your feelings. They spring from your heart. If it is regret you feel, face it. Acknowledge it. Understand it. Realize that it is a natural response to the death of someone you've known and loved.

"If it is guilt you feel, take charge of it. Know that nothing you may have done or said could in any way force Chad to take the steps he took. The Chad we knew didn't take his life. By the time he reached the desperate point at which he decided to end his own life, the Chad we knew no longer existed. Chad was not seeking to end his life, but to end his pain.

"Despite the tragedy that has occurred, I am here to tell you that all is not lost. This is not the end of your world, though at the moment it might seem that way. We must use this tragic, unexpected turn of events to give us new understanding and compassion for the needs and desires of others, their strengths and weaknesses, their vulnerabilities—and our own.

"Family and friends, this is a time when we must all cast ourselves upon the grace and mercy of our God. Chad is His responsibility now."

Lexi caught a glimpse of Chad's parents out of the corner of her eye and her heart grieved for them.

Pastor Horace continued, "Chad struggled in his life. But struggle is not unusual, nor was it unique to Chad. Even St. Paul in the book of Romans talks of his own struggles with life. He says, 'Sin rules me as if I were a slave. I do not understand the things I do. I do not do the good things I want to do and I do the bad things I hate to do. But I am not really the one who is doing these hated things. It is sin living in me that does these things. Yes, I know that nothing good lives in me, I mean nothing good lives in the part of me that is earthly and sinful. . . .

" 'So I have learned this rule: When I want to do good, evil is there with me. In my mind, I am happy with God's law. But I see another law working in my body. That law makes war against the law that my mind accepts. That other law working in my body is the law of sin, and that law makes me its prisoner. What a miserable man I am! Who will save me from this body that brings me death? God will. I thank him for saving me through Jesus Christ, our Lord!'

"If a great man of the Bible can have such a struggle, is it surprising that many of us have struggles too? Now is the time to call upon God's comfort and help, for He understands."

Lexi glanced around at her friends. Everyone was intent on the pastor's exhortation.

"It is important to emphasize that Paul continues on in the next chapter, rejoicing over our new life through the Holy Spirit. He says, 'Therefore, there is now no condemnation for those who are in Christ Jesus, because through Christ Jesus the law of the Spirit of life set me free from the law of sin and death.' We must all learn to deal with Chad's death in our own way. In our own time. God's gift to us is life. We, as survivors, must cherish it even more fully now.

"I'd like to speak particularly to you young people. Your friend has committed suicide. You feel desperate and alone. But it is comforting to know that even Jesus had the experience you are having right now. Judas, his confidant, one of his chosen, also committed suicide. *You are not alone.* Jesus Christ understands you more fully than you can possibly know."

Lexi was increasingly amazed at Pastor Horace's insight, and was thankful she had not stayed home and missed his message.

"At a time like this, you may even wonder if your own lives are worth living, if it's worth going on. I say an emphatic 'Yes!' Your life *is* worth living! God has many years planned for you. Just because we know God and believe in Him doesn't mean we'll be free from trouble or disappointment in our lives. What it does mean, however, is that He is willing to go through all our problems and our trials with us. He's always there for us. All we have to do is call on His name. Once we know that He's there, we can move from despair and hopelessness to anticipation and hope for the future."

Then the pastor's expression grew light, almost joyous.

"We should be asking ourselves why it is we are to *live* rather than if we should die. Suicide can't answer any of your questions. God can. I emphasize to you, young people, there is no problem that you cannot face with God's help. Pray to God and wait for His answer. Listen to His voice. You need not be lost in this life. You need not be alone. God will be with you always. Amen."

There was a hush over the congregation at the close of the pastor's remarks. At the end of the service, Lexi and her friends met outside the church. Binky's and Jennifer's faces were red and swollen from crying. Even Egg's nose was pink and puffy. And Todd's eyes were glazed with tears.

Mrs. Leighton put her arms around Binky and Jennifer. "Why don't you young folks come over to our place for a while? I don't imagine any of you feel much like being alone right now."

Everyone nodded their agreement and headed for the Leightons'. As they gathered silently around the kitchen table, each was lost in their own thoughts and grief. For the first time, Lexi felt like she was unable to reach out to any of them.

"Why didn't he *say* something?" Egg finally blurted, his eyes showing his anguish. "Why didn't he tell one of us how unhappy he was?"

"Maybe he tried and we didn't listen," Binky whimpered.

"I don't think he *could* tell us how he felt," Todd said softly.

"If he *had* been able to tell us, would we have understood? Would we have listened?" Jennifer's voice was shaking.

"I wish we could do this over," Binky wailed. "I'd be so different the second time around. I'd watch out for Chad. I'd listen to him. I'd be his friend."

"But we're not going to get to do this over, Binky. When there's a suicide, there's no turning back. You don't get another chance."

That's what hurt most of all. Chad was gone and there was no one who could bring him back.

As they contemplated the sad fact, Ben walked into the kitchen and looked at each one curiously.

"I feel so awful." Jennifer rocked back and forth in her chair. "I wish there was something I could do."

Ben peered at her, his eyes wide with wonder.

"I saw Chad every day and I didn't help him at all." Egg gave a weepy snort. "I just figured he'd have to work his problems out with Peggy. I never even dreamed—"

"Does anyone want to play kickball with me?" Ben interrupted sweetly.

Egg looked at him blankly. "Not now, Ben. Maybe later."

"But I've got the ball out now. Do you want to play kickball with me, Todd?"

Todd tried to smile. "I've got a lot on my mind, Ben. I don't think I would be much fun."

"How about you, Lexi? Will you play with me?" Ben was getting frustrated.

"I don't think so, sweetie. Why don't you go outside and practice. You can play by yourself for a while."

"Good idea, Ben," Binky said. "Run along now."

Ben stood in the center of the kitchen floor, his hands on his hips. He stared at the group huddled around the kitchen table. His lip turned down in a frown and his eyebrows furrowed together over the bridge of his nose. "Quit trying to send me away!" he protested. "I want to play kickball."

"Ben, you don't understand. We have something very important on our minds right now," Lexi explained.

Ben nodded his head emphatically. "Ben understands. Ben knows."

"No you don't, Ben."

"Yes I do. You're sad because Chad's dead."

Lexi gasped, and her friends looked astonished at Ben's pronouncement.

There was a disgruntled look on Ben's face. "But Chad belongs to God now. Let God worry about Chad. *You* play with *me!*"

Todd shifted uncomfortably in his chair. "Ben's right, you know. That's what Pastor Horace said. Chad belongs to God now. His fate is in God's hands, not ours."

"Life goes on," Jennifer added. "That's what he was trying to tell us."

Binky chewed on her lower lip. "I suppose it would be healthier for us to pay attention to Ben. He's the one who needs us now. Instead of sitting here feeling guilty about the things we didn't do for Chad, maybe we should start doing something for other people."

Ben's statement had been something of a revelation. Slowly, painfully, the healing process had begun.

———

The next afternoon Lexi was surprised to see Peggy Madison coming down the sidewalk toward her house. Lexi met her at the door. "Peggy. Come in." Peggy had been in great pain and distress the last few days. She was pale and her hands trembled almost imperceptibly. "Sit down, Peggy. I'm glad you came."

Peggy sank against the couch in the Leighton living room and threw her head backward, closing her eyes. Two tears managed to squeeze from beneath her eyelids. "I couldn't stay home, Lexi. I had to come. I hope you don't mind."

"Mind? Of course not. I'm here for you anytime."

"That's because you're a true friend, Lexi. I wasn't Chad's friend. I wasn't there for him. And look what happened." Guilt and regret seasoned Peggy's words. "He was wrong, Lexi, wrong to kill himself! I think he meant to punish me—and he did. Now all I have left is a horrible sense of guilt. If I'd done something differently, Chad might be alive today. That's what he wanted me to think. How could he do that to me?" Peggy grimaced. "Maybe I should do the same thing Chad did. I've ruined my life anyway."

"No, Peggy." Lexi tried to be firm, hoping Peggy wouldn't sense how afraid she felt for her. "Don't talk like that."

Peggy blinked, startled at her own words and Lexi's response. "I know. I didn't mean it, Lexi. It was a stupid thing to say. It's just that I feel so *guilty*. I keep asking myself if Chad's death was my fault. I keep thinking that I could have prevented it. I knew how depressed he was. I knew how much he wanted to talk to me. Why didn't I talk to him the other night at the football game? Maybe if I'd just talked to him that one time . . ."

"You can't know that, Peggy. You're just guessing. Chad's mind might have been made up a long time ago. You can't think that you might have changed anything."

Peggy gave her an anguished look. "How am I ever going to get over this, Lexi? How?"

"My mom says you can't really get over it. You can only learn how to deal with it. It's not going to go away."

"I get so mixed up. My feelings are so confused. Sometimes I feel so guilty I think I'm going to explode and then, just when I don't think I can stand it anymore, I realize how angry I am at Chad. How could he do this to us?"

Just then Mrs. Leighton walked into the living room. It was obvious to Lexi that her mother had overheard Peggy's last words. "Peggy," she began, "you might think that I'm intruding on your conversation, but I have something that I'd like to give you."

Peggy looked startled. "Oh? What's that, Mrs. Leighton?"

She went to her desk and pulled out a journal. Her mother had written in journals for as long as Lexi could remember. She called them her "everyday diaries."

"I'd like you to have this."

Peggy hesitated, then took the floral-patterned book.

"It's a journal, Peggy. Lexi can tell you that I write in mine every day. I picked this one up the last time I was at the stationery store. I think you need it more than I do."

"Why would I need it?" Peggy asked skeptically. "I'm not much for writing."

"I want you to do me a favor. Write down everything you're feeling these days. Putting it down on paper helps. It might even be good if you wrote a letter to Chad."

"A letter?" Peggy laughed bitterly. "Chad can't read a letter now."

"Of course not, Peggy, but you can express the feelings you have. Empty yourself onto the page. Get rid of the guilt and anger you feel by writing it out. Write down what you'd like to say to Chad, all that you didn't have the opportunity to say before, including goodbye. You can't carry all these emotions around inside. The pressure will build and build until it boils over. I know journaling may sound strange to you right now, but will you try it for me?"

Peggy clutched the notebook more firmly. "All right, Mrs. Leighton. For you, I'll try."

"Good." She patted Peggy's arm and rose to leave. "Oh, and one more thing. I'd like to call your mother and suggest that she get in touch with a support group."

"What's that?" Peggy looked suspicious.

"There are support groups organized for people whose loved ones have committed suicide. I think you and your parents should consider going to some of their meetings, Peggy. You will meet others who have had a similar experience to yours."

"Others? Like me?" Peggy was surprised.

"Chad isn't the first person ever to commit suicide nor, unfortunately, will he be the last. Support groups are for the survivors. It teaches them how to cope. Would you consider a group like that, Peggy?"

"I don't know. Would I have to talk to strangers?"

"Probably. But you'd most likely get to know them well enough before you are asked to share your experience."

"Well, maybe," Peggy said, a little unsure. "I could try it—once."

Mrs. Leighton nodded. "I'm glad, Peggy."

"Sit down, Mom," Lexi spoke up. "Maybe you can help answer some questions for us."

"I'm not sure I understand anything anymore," Peggy admitted. "I just keep asking myself, 'Why, Chad? Why?' "

Mrs. Leighton sat down next to her daughter and tucked her feet beneath her. "Chad's self-esteem was at a low ebb. Self-worth is not something that is gained overnight anyway. After years of not feeling worthy Chad came to the end of himself. When things didn't go well for him, he didn't know how to cope because he didn't value his own ability to go on." Mrs. Leighton seemed wise beyond her years. "What happened between you at the football game the other night couldn't have been the deciding factor for Chad. Momentum for his fateful decision had been building for many years.

"Unfortunately, we're all partly to blame. We should all be looking out for young people like Chad who need affirmation, who need to know they're special and they're loved."

"I still think it's my fault," Peggy said stubbornly, her chin trembling.

"Peggy, do you mind if we pray for you?" Mrs. Leighton asked abruptly.

Peggy nodded, and Mrs. Leighton reached for her hand. Lexi took her mother's, and she began: "Dear Heavenly Father. As you know, Peggy is feeling a great deal of guilt over the death of her friend. Please comfort her, Lord, and take this guilt from her heart. Help her to forgive herself and to forgive Chad. Help her to know that she's not alone with her feelings. Tell her how much she is loved by all of us. We all need your love and understanding now, Lord. We're like dry sponges ready to soak up your goodness and mercy. Shower us with your blessing and care, Lord, and with your strength. We are weak and very much in need. Amen."

Peggy smiled through her tears and thanked Lexi and her mother for their care and concern for her. When she left a short time later, Lexi stood watching her friend as she walked slowly toward home.

What's next? Will Peggy ever be able to cope with her loss?

Chapter Nine

"No matter how long I live or how hard I try, I'll never forget.

"My mother came into my room to wake me up and she looked as though she'd been crying. I could tell by her expression that something was wrong. Terribly, terribly wrong. I thought maybe something had happened to Daddy or to someone else in my family.

"It's funny, really, but just looking at her face made my stomach feel as though someone had kicked me hard, with a booted foot. But it wasn't Daddy. It was Chad. Mother told me he was dead.

"I knew immediately that he'd killed himself, even before she told me. I don't know how I knew. I just did. I suppose, deep down inside, I wasn't even surprised. Still, I told her I didn't believe her, that she was wrong, that there'd been a mistake. She started crying too. She held me in her arms and rocked me just as she did when I was a child.

"I kept shaking my head and saying 'no, no, no,' when inside I was terrified and my brain was screaming 'yes, yes, yes.' I told Mom that it was my fault Chad

105

had died; that if it hadn't been for me, none of this would have happened. If I'd agreed to go out with him again, if I'd even talked to him, he might never have done this terrible thing. Mom didn't agree with me. She said that I couldn't be responsible for what someone else did. She said blaming myself was a serious mistake. I didn't believe her, but she insisted that it was true.

"She said she thought Chad had done something impulsive, not realizing that his actions would be so permanent. I remember her using that word. Permanent.

"Permanent means forever. That's how long Chad will be gone. Forever. I'll never see him again. I'll never hear his voice. I'll never touch his hand. I loved him once. We had a baby together—and now he's gone forever. It can't get more permanent than that.

"Lexi's mom told me I should keep this journal. She said it would be good for me to get my thoughts and feelings out on paper. I didn't believe her at first, but took the journal just to be polite. But, you know, I think she's right. It helps to say all these things to someone, even if it is just a piece of paper in a book.

"Lexi's been great. She's trying to help, but no one can know exactly how I feel, unless they've been through this themselves. There's not a minute goes by that I don't think about Chad. Something always reminds me of him. First the good times, then the bad. Will there ever be a day when life seems normal again? It doesn't seem possible now, but my friends say it's out there, I just have to find it."

———

It was amazing to Lexi that despite what had

happened, life went on more or less as usual. Although the teachers were sympathetic and willing to listen whenever a student had questions or fears, classes continued on schedule.

"In a way, it's a good thing we have to keep busy," Egg said one afternoon as they all sat in the *Cedar River Review* newsroom. "I think I'd lose my mind if I didn't have other things to think about."

Todd waved a photo negative in the air to dry. "I know what you mean, Egg. Fortunately, the *Cedar River Review* has to get out on time. I guess that means Lexi does the photos and captions no matter what happens."

Lexi looked up from the paper she was working on. "My heart isn't in it, though. I used to have fun with this." She stared at a picture of the girl's basketball team. "Today I feel like I'm just putting down words to get the job done."

Egg shrugged. "Well, at least you have some words to put down. I'm still missing Minda Hannaford's fashion column."

Just then the door flew open and slammed against the wall. Minda stood in the frame a moment, then entered the room. Instead of her usual sharp remark, she grabbed the doorknob and closed the door quietly behind her. She sat down between Lexi and Todd.

"We were just talking about you," Egg said. "Where's the column?"

"It's almost done, Egg. Don't pop a vessel over it."

Egg glanced at his watch. "Oh, I won't. Glad to hear it's almost done. Isn't it about time to get ready for football practice, Todd?"

Todd pushed away from the table and stood. "See you girls later."

Lexi waved goodbye and smiled at Todd.

Contrary to her style, Minda ignored the boys and remained seated.

Lexi was surprised. Normally Minda showed little interest in spending any time with Lexi.

"I want to talk to you," Minda said bluntly.

"Oh, what about?"

"How's Peggy Madison doing?" Minda asked.

It seemed like a reasonable question, but usually Minda only cared about her own little group of friends. "She's doing okay, under the circumstances."

Minda gave her a knowing look. "Well, I've been worried about her. She walks through the halls looking like a ghost. I've tried to talk to her, but she hardly seems to be there."

"I know what you mean," Lexi admitted. "She scares me sometimes. I try to keep in touch with her every day and I've talked to her mother quite a bit."

"And?" Minda looked genuinely concerned. For once, Lexi believed that Minda was sincere.

"She's having a tough time dealing with the fact that Chad is actually gone. She's nervous as a cat. Any little sound makes her jump. And she seems to be fascinated with anything that has to do with death."

"It's morbid, if you ask me."

"I was watching her in history class one day. They were talking about the assassination of one of the presidents. I could just see Peggy's mind click on. It was as if everything that was said reminded her of Chad."

"I can't imagine how she's managing to get her homework done."

"I don't know how she's doing it either," Lexi said. "Her mother says she sleeps a lot. She really doesn't seek out any of her friends. Sometimes I think we're just a reminder of her loss, Minda. When she sees us she remembers the things that we've done together as a class. Then she remembers Chad. I hate to add to her unhappiness, but I don't want to leave her alone either."

"Well, if you can't figure out what to do, I guess there's no hope for me then," Minda said dejectedly.

"What do you mean?"

"You and Peggy are close friends. Peggy and I have never been close. We actually haven't even liked each other. When I see her walking around so pale and miserable, it makes me feel like I should do something."

"That's very nice of you, Minda," Lexi said, genuinely impressed. "Perhaps it would help just to tell Peggy that you're worried about her."

"Do you think she'd actually believe me?" Minda asked with a light laugh. "I've done some pretty rotten things to Peggy in my time." Minda probably referred to the time when, in the *Cedar River Review*, she'd hinted at the pregnancy of a high school girl.

"Forget the past, Minda. This is a new day. People can start over. People can change."

"You really believe that don't you, Leighton," Minda said.

"Yes, I do."

"You're strange, Lexi, but you're all right," Minda said bluntly. She rose from the table. "I've never been able to figure you out, but I think, just maybe, that I'm beginning to."

Minda looked suddenly wise for her age. "Chad's death has reminded me that life's pretty precious. It probably shouldn't be spent making enemies. We'd be better off making friends." Minda glanced at the clock on the wall. "Gotta go. See you later."

When Lexi smiled and nodded, Minda returned the smile. After she left, Lexi rested her head on her hands and stared at the closed door. Her mind reeled. Had it been a dream or had it really happened? Was a new bond forming between Minda and her?

––––––––

"It seems like a hundred years since we were last at a football game instead of just days," Binky observed as they sat on the bleachers watching the Cedar River Cougars.

Lexi tipped her head back and took a deep breath of the crisp fall air. "Feels good, doesn't it? It feels normal to be out here watching the game. That's what teenagers should be doing, instead of thinking about dying and losing their friends."

"It's funny," Binky mused, "but, when I wake up in the morning, I'm amazed at how ordinary everything seems. For some reason, after Chad died, I thought that nothing would ever be the same again. It is though, isn't it?"

"Life goes on. That's what my dad keeps telling me."

"I guess he's right, but I wish Chad were here to enjoy it," Binky's eyes were downcast for a moment. "Still, one thing I've learned is never to take other people for granted. To never assume you know what they're thinking. And never to be unkind."

"I guess Chad gave you a pretty special gift, didn't he, Binky?"

Binky paused to consider. She nodded slowly. "He sure did."

A sudden moan arose from the crowd, drawing Lexi's and Binky's attention back to the playing field.

Jennifer whistled through her teeth. "Boy, Todd really got sacked that time! Did you see how hard he went down?"

Everyone stood, all eyes focused on the playing field.

"Did he get hurt?" Binky asked, fear slicing through her. Lexi clutched her box of popcorn and stared with her mouth open. Todd was on his back, unmoving. Lexi saw that the coach and Egg were becoming restless on the sidelines. Moments passed.

Finally, Todd moved. Then he sat up, pulled off his helmet and shook his head. With the help of one of his teammates, he rose to his feet and gave a victory sign to the crowd. Everyone cheered, and Lexi sank down on the bleachers, her heart pounding. "Oh, Todd Winston, don't scare me like that!"

Jennifer's eyes were large and round. "It took him forever to get up."

"Do you think he's all right?" Binky asked, her face creased with worry.

"He looks fine to me," Jennifer said. "And he's going to keep playing."

"He must be all right then," Lexi said. "But the time he was on the ground did seem like forever."

Lexi was restless, wishing the game would end. She wanted to talk to Todd, to see for herself that he was really all right. A Cedar River victory couldn't come too quickly for her tonight.

In the fourth quarter, the "quarterback sneak" was the play that cinched the game. Todd, ball in hand, tucked his head and dived over the center, breaking through the defensive line and scoring the final touchdown. Cedar River had won again.

After the game, as she and her friends stood together waiting for Todd, Lexi shifted her feet nervously. "What're they doing in there? Do you think Todd's all right?"

"He's fine, Lexi. I talked to Egg. Todd just got the wind knocked out of him, that's all."

Todd came meandering from the locker room with Egg, deep in a discussion over the last play of the game. Lexi ran to him and threw her arms around him. "Todd, are you all right?" She nearly knocked him off balance.

"You're more dangerous than the guys on the football field, Lexi. I'm *expecting* them to tackle me."

"Are you okay? Are you sure you're okay?"

"Hey, I'm just fine. I got the wind knocked out of me, that's all." Todd laughed and joked. He casually brushed a strand of hair from Lexi's eyes. No matter how normally he was behaving, Lexi felt queasy inside. Ever since Chad's death, she'd begun to realize just how important Todd was to her. The thought of him being hurt sent a bolt of panic through her.

"Anybody hungry?" Todd asked the group. He rubbed his stomach. "I'm starved. How about something at the Hamburger Shack?"

"Sounds good to me," Egg agreed.

"Do you mind if we stop by Peggy's house and pick her up?" Lexi asked. "She didn't want to come to the game, but I told her we might go out afterward. Maybe she'd like to come."

"Of course," Todd said. Everyone chorused their approval. They'd become protective of Peggy these days.

Peggy was sitting on the porch steps when they reached the Madisons'. She looked weary, but smiled when she saw her friends. "Who won the game?" she asked.

"Cedar River, who else?" Todd called.

"Thanks to our quarterback," Jennifer added. "We're going to the Hamburger Shack, Peggy. Can you come?"

A look of indecision registered on Peggy's face. Then she saw Lexi. "Well, I suppose I could."

Lexi knew how difficult it was for Peggy to be out in public. She imagined that people assumed she was the cause of Chad's death.

Everyone entered their familiar eating place and claimed a booth at the back. Todd studied the menu as if he'd never seen it before. "I didn't have much to eat before the game. I think I could order everything on the menu."

"You aren't serious are you?" Lexi laughed.

When Jerry Randall came to their table, Todd ordered first: "Three cheeseburgers, a double order of fries and a chocolate shake. That should be enough to start."

Egg, who could eat twenty-four hours a day and still not gain a pound, ordered a shrimp basket and a strawberry sundae.

The girls smiled and ordered beverages and a large order of fries to split. While they were waiting for their food, Todd and Egg spoke animatedly of the game play by play.

Egg slapped his palm on the table. "I wish Chad could have seen that last play. That was something—" He froze mid-sentence.

It had become an unspoken rule not to mention Chad's name in Peggy's presence. Egg had inadvertently touched the tender spot. He swallowed deeply, causing his Adam's apple to bob.

Peggy clenched the spoon in her hand. "You don't have to worry about saying his name around me, Egg. I know you're all tiptoeing around, as if you'll hurt me by speaking of Chad. I wish you'd stop it. I'm not a baby. I don't need to be protected." She dropped the spoon on the table and held her face in her hands. "What is it about me?"

"Huh?" Egg said blankly.

"First Chad tries to punish me by doing the worst possible thing he could do to himself. Now, you're all acting like I'm a keg of dynamite about to go off." Her eyes glossed with tears. "How could Chad do this to me? How could he want to hurt me so badly? Why did he want to ruin my life as well as his own?" She was shaking like a leaf now.

Todd reached across the table and took Peggy's wrists in his hands. "Don't do this to yourself," he said firmly, forcing her to look into his eyes.

"Do what?" she retorted. "Isn't it that things are being done to me? I feel like I'm the victim."

"Maybe you are in a way," Todd said. "We all realize that you feel badly, Peggy. So do we. Chad was our friend, and we miss him too, but don't you think it's time you made some choices?"

"Choices?" Peggy looked puzzled.

"It seems to me you have a choice to make right now. You can either choose to allow Chad's death to destroy you, to take you down the same path he followed. Or, you can choose *life*. Learn something from Chad's death. Don't waste it. Find some meaning in it—a purpose for your own life. It's up to you."

Peggy was silent. Todd's hands were still wrapped around her wrists. He released them gently.

"I guess I never really thought about it like that before," she said quietly.

"We all love you, Peggy," Todd continued, "but we have to go on. We want to help you but your new life has to start with you."

Chapter Ten

Lexi and Ben were playing a game of checkers when the telephone rang. "I'll get it," Ben volunteered. He jumped up from his chair so quickly he nearly knocked it over. Picking up the receiver carefully, he said, "Leighton residence. Ben speaking. May I help you?"

Ever since the afternoon Lexi had allowed Ben to help her answer the telephone at their father's veterinary clinic, Ben had been very business-like and self-confident on the phone.

"It's for you, Lexi." He thrust the receiver in her direction. "Somebody's sad."

Lexi knew immediately who that would be.

"What are you doing, Lexi?" Peggy's voice was weak and distant.

"Playing checkers with Ben. I'm getting whomped."

"Oh, that's nice."

"Nice that I'm playing checkers or that I'm getting whomped?" Lexi asked. She found herself often making an effort to tease Peggy out of her depression. So far, she hadn't met with much success. "What are you doing?"

"Nothing."

117

Lexi knew that statement was all too true. Peggy spent much of her time sitting in her room in a rocker, staring out the window. Her grades had fallen off. Even though her teachers were sympathetic, they were becoming frustrated with Peggy's lack of effort to come back to reality.

"Why don't you come over here?" Lexi suggested. "Maybe you can beat Ben at a game of checkers."

"I doubt that. He wouldn't want to play with me, anyway."

"Don't be silly. You're one of his favorite people in the whole world. We don't have to play checkers, either. We could make brownies or listen to music."

"Sounds like a lot of work."

"To walk over here? Come on, Peggy. We're practically next-door neighbors! Do you want me to come and get you?"

"No, but it'll be ten minutes, at least. I'm not dressed yet."

Lexi looked at her watch. It was two o'clock on a Saturday afternoon and Peggy wasn't dressed! She shook her head in bewilderment.

"All right. See you soon. Hurry over." Lexi hung up the phone. When she returned to the checkerboard, Ben was busy stacking the checkers in red and black piles.

"I won!" he announced cheerfully.

"You might have," Lexi agreed, "but you haven't yet."

"All done." Ben gave her a gleeful smile.

"You do love to win, don't you Ben."

Ben nodded his head enthusiastically. "Everybody likes to win."

"Yeah. Me too. Sometime I want you to *let* me win."

Ben covered his mouth and chuckled. "You're a big girl, Lexi. Do it yourself." He gathered up his checkerboard game and left the room.

"Are you two finished playing already?" Mrs. Leighton came in from working in the yard.

"The little pirate was beating me again."

"So what else is new?" Mrs. Leighton laughed as she washed her hands.

"I've invited Peggy to come over."

"Good. I was talking to Mrs. Madison the other day. She's very worried about Peggy."

"She has every right to be," Lexi said bluntly. "Mom, there's something I need to talk to you about."

"What is it, dear?" Mrs. Leighton dried her hands and perched on the edge of a stool.

"I don't think Peggy's snapping back quickly enough after Chad's death."

"It's a great deal to expect, Lexi."

"I realize that, but I think it's more serious than just depression." Lexi paused, trying to form in her mind the next statement. "Mom, I think Peggy might be considering suicide."

Mrs. Leighton's nodded. "Peggy's mother is concerned about the same thing. They're seeking more counseling for her."

"Is there anything I can do, Mom? Is there anything I could say that might help her?"

"It's quite a responsibility, Lexi. I'm sure you can encourage her and spend time with her, but I think she needs professional help right now."

"But what if she doesn't want to talk to professionals?"

"I never thought of that. Do you think Peggy would talk to me?"

Lexi nodded enthusiastically. "I'm sure she would, Mom. She thinks you're great. She remembers how kind you were to her when she was pregnant. You never condemned her, you just loved her."

"Maybe the three of us could have a little conversation this afternoon when she comes." Mrs. Leighton smiled and patted Lexi's hand.

Before long, Peggy was at the door. Lexi tried not to look too shocked at her friend's appearance. She wore a drab gray sweatsuit. Her hair was uncombed and she wasn't wearing any makeup.

"I suppose I look like I just crawled out of bed," Peggy said by way of apology.

Mrs. Leighton hugged her spontaneously. "You look fine to me, Peggy. Come and sit down in the living room."

"You're always so nice to me, Mrs. Leighton." Peggy looked at Lexi's mom as if she wanted to ask why.

"I suppose it's because I like you, Peggy. I love you, actually."

Peggy looked as if she might cry. "Could we talk? I guess everyone is probably tired of my talking about Chad's death, but I'm still having trouble with it." Peggy sank into a chair. "People seem concerned and want to help, but no one answers my questions. I'm not getting any straight answers, Mrs. Leighton. Can you help me?"

Lexi took a chair opposite, and her mother sat

down next to Peggy. "That's a pretty big request. I don't know if I can be of help. I'm not a counselor, Peggy."

"It doesn't matter. You'll be honest with me, won't you?"

"Of course, Peggy. And I'm happy to answer your questions the best I can. But I don't have all the answers. I have opinions, which can be right or wrong."

"That's good enough for me."

"Fine. Are you comfortable in that chair, Peggy?"

"It's okay." She tucked her feet beneath her and wrapped her arms around herself.

"Are you cold?"

"I'm always cold."

Lexi pulled an afghan from behind the recliner. "Here, wrap up in this." It was a big fluffy blanket that her Grandma Carson had crocheted. "You look so cozy, I think I'll get one for myself."

Mrs. Leighton had gone into the kitchen and returned with a bowl of caramel corn. Both girls were curled up in the blankets. "It's a good thing my mother loved to crochet," she said. She reached behind the couch and pulled out a third afghan. "There now, are we ready to talk?"

Quite unexpectedly, Peggy blurted, "Mrs. Leighton, will you tell me what the Bible says about suicide?"

Lexi's mom reached for her well-worn Bible. "You really know how to ask the tough ones, don't you, Peggy?"

"No one ever tells me what the Bible says." Peggy sounded frustrated.

"You know what Pastor Horace said at the funeral."

"Yes, but there must be more."

"Well, the Bible does say we should try to prevent people from taking their own lives. In Proverbs 24 it says, 'Save those who are being led to their death. Rescue those who are about to be killed.' God doesn't want anyone to die unnecessarily. Sadly, suicide is one of biggest killers of young people in our country today. Beautiful lives are being snuffed out." Mrs. Leighton leaned her head against the back of the chair in thought. "I've wondered if we could have read Chad's mood if we'd been wiser about these things," she admitted. "I've also thought the teachers at school should attend seminars that deal with suicidal students."

"How would a teacher know they're suicidal?" Peggy asked.

"One signal is when a student is preoccupied with death. He either talks about it all the time or writes about it in his theme papers. The *idea* of suicide is like a seed planted in the ground. If a student is lonely, depressed or unhappy with his life, that seed finds fertile ground to take root and grow.

"As Christians, we shouldn't allow negative thoughts to remain in our minds. Instead, we should refuse them, and choose to fill our mind with good things. There's a verse in Philippians 4 that says, 'Continue to think about the things that are good and worthy of praise. Think about the things that are true and honorable and right and pure and beautiful and respected.' Those are the thoughts we should be dwelling on, not negative ideas that deal with death or destruction."

Mrs. Leighton glanced at Lexi. "Lexi knows what I'm talking about. Binky went through a time when all she could think about was horror movies. She had to learn the hard way that that kind of input is harmful."

"I'm not sure I understand or agree with you, Mrs. Leighton," Peggy said frankly. "It's unrealistic to always fill your mind with good thoughts. What is wrong with thinking occasionally about death? Our body is our own, isn't it? I know it's wrong to cause the death of someone else, but is it wrong to make a decision about your *own* body?"

Lexy could tell her Mom was praying for wisdom in answering Peggy's difficult question.

"I don't believe our body *is* completely our own." Mrs. Leighton continued. "Jesus Christ paid a high price on the cross for each one of us. Our bodies really belong to Him. There's a verse in First Corinthians that says, 'You should know that your body is the temple of the Holy Spirit. The Holy Spirit is in you. You have received the Holy Spirit from God. You do not own yourself. You were bought by God for a price.' "

"So my body doesn't really belong to me?"

"Not entirely, Peggy. When someone commits suicide, they destroy the temple which is God's, and for which he shed His own blood. The Bible tells us to preserve and take care of our bodies for Him, not to harm them."

Peggy didn't seem convinced. "I hear what you're saying, but sometimes I think death is the end of everything. I wonder if we really do go on—to live with God, I mean." Peggy looked down at the floor.

"I'm ashamed to admit that. But I have so many doubts."

Mrs. Leighton laid her hand on Peggy's arm. "We're all human, Peggy. All of us have doubts from time to time. I respect you for being honest and for trying to get answers to your questions. But death really is not the end for the Christian. It's only the beginning. First we will stand before God in judgment."

"Do you mean that someone shouldn't commit suicide because they'll have to face God?" A panicked expression spread over Peggy's face. "What about Chad? Does God condemn him for what he did?"

"To answer your first question, Peggy, everyone has to face God when they die, not just those who commit suicide. And remember what Pastor Horace said. Chad is in God's hands now. God is a just God and He will do what is right. He is also a God of love and mercy. He alone knew Chad's heart, his motives. We have to trust God to take everything into account and make the wisest and most loving judgment. There's nothing that we can do or say that will change the outcome."

"I want to believe what you're saying, Mrs. Leighton," Peggy said quietly.

"I'm glad for that, Peggy. But doubting is part of human nature too. God doesn't judge us for doubting. He is very patient with us. Sometimes, when your prayers seem to be falling on deaf ears, it's easy to be discouraged, but God is listening, whether you think so or not."

Peggy was struggling to understand all that Mrs. Leighton was telling her. "It's just so complicated.

Honestly, Mrs. Leighton, sometimes in the past few weeks, I've thought that Chad had the right idea. To just end it all. To end the pain."

"But remember what I said, Peggy. Death is not the end. It's the beginning. It's far better to face death with anticipation, to look forward to spending eternity with your Heavenly Father than to view death as a blank, as a void. Besides that, our bodies aren't our own. We can't do with them what we please."

"I understand about Christ dying for us and all that, but I still think my body is *my* body."

Mrs. Leighton turned to her Bible again and thumbed through the pages. "Listen to this verse from Romans 12:5: 'In the same way, we are many, but in Christ we are all one body. Each one is a part of that body and each part belongs to all the other parts.' "

"But that's just one verse."

Peggy's words were a challenge to Mrs. Leighton who loved to study the Bible.

"Okay. Here's another verse in 1 Corinthians 15: 'Surely you know that your bodies are parts of Christ himself.' It says again in Ephesians that we are parts of His body. And Romans 14 is a particular favorite: 'For we do not live or die for ourselves. If we live we are living for the Lord and if we die, we are dying for the Lord, so living or dying, we belong to the Lord.'

"When someone attempts suicide, they personally hurt the body of Christ, Peggy. If you cut your hand, you feel the pain throughout your entire body, not just in your hand. It's the same way with a suicide. The community of mankind is diminished each time someone takes their own life."

"You mean that each one of us is so important to Christ that we're like a part of His body?"

"That's exactly what I mean, Peggy. To commit suicide is like turning a knife on God's own body and slicing a portion of it away. When Chad killed himself because he was trying to end his own pain, we inherited his pain. We're all a part of one body—that of mankind, that of Christ."

Peggy wrapped the afghan more tightly around her shoulders. "You two are the first people I've told that I've wanted to commit suicide," Peggy admitted. "I wouldn't have dared tell my mother or my father. They would have freaked."

"Perhaps, perhaps not," Mrs. Leighton said calmly. "I think you should trust them more, Peggy. They've seen that you are in trouble. They've been worried about you. Your mother said they were seeking a counselor for you, someone who could help you through this. Why don't you go home and tell them what you've told us?"

Peggy seemed surprised to know that her parents were so tuned in to her situation.

"Don't be shocked, Peggy," Mrs. Leighton patted her hand. "Parents aren't as dumb as you think. In fact, sometimes they're really quite wise. But, if there's a time when you can't talk to your parents, you know that you're always free to come here and talk to me, Jim or Lexi. Just call. Don't hesitate."

"Sometimes I feel like such a pest." Tears came to Peggy's eyes.

"You're never a pest. Not to us. Not to anyone. And don't be afraid to cry either. Tears are good,

Peggy. It's nature's way of cleansing."

"Well, I've cried enough," Peggy admitted.

"You'll make it through this. I have no doubt."

"I wish I didn't have any doubt," Peggy said.

"Day by day, things will get a little easier. It won't happen overnight or even in a matter of weeks. It may take months, but you *will* heal and you *will* survive."

"But I drive myself crazy asking *why* this had to happen, Mrs. Leighton."

"That's okay. Keep asking. Once you've formed a satisfactory answer, you'll be able to put it behind you. Chad was a hurting, unhappy boy. Although you were involved with him, you did not intentionally cause his pain. Remember that."

"But I feel so *low*."

"Yes, and sometimes you'll feel high. It's all right. It's normal, Peggy. You've been through a terrible ordeal. When you have any feelings, express them. Don't bottle them up inside. You may feel angry with Chad, angry with God. Feel free to express that. Speak it out. Be honest with yourself and with others. Honesty doesn't hurt anyone. It's dishonesty, particularly lying to yourself, that does."

"I'd like to lie to myself, Mrs. Leighton," Peggy admitted. "I'd like to think that I didn't have anything to do with Chad's wanting to commit suicide, but I know I did. He wanted me to date him again. He wanted to go back to where we were before the baby, but I just couldn't."

"And you were right, Peggy. Chad was expecting more of you than you had to give. Never feel guilty for turning your own life around. Don't feel guilty for refusing to fall back into a trap that would have hurt you. Chad shouldn't have been trying to live in the past, Peggy. That was part of his problem. *His problem*, not yours."

Peggy rubbed her eyes. "I don't know. Maybe you're right, Mrs. Leighton. Maybe suicide isn't such a good idea."

"No it isn't. You *will* make it, Peggy. You'll go through all of this and come out a stronger and a better person than you ever thought possible. You will even laugh again."

Peggy looked startled. "How did you know that I haven't been able to laugh?"

"It's only natural. Nothing's seemed funny to you or laughable for a very long time." Mrs. Leighton smiled knowingly. "With friends like Binky and Egg I think there will be some laughter in the future no matter how hard you try to avoid it."

Peggy smiled in spite of herself. "I guess you're right. I want to thank you Mrs. Leighton, and you too, Lexi, for listening to me. You've given me some things to think about other than my own problems. And I will call if I need to talk again." She rose to leave, and Mrs. Leighton and Lexi saw her to the door.

Lexi hugged her friend and promised to see her soon.

After Peggy had gone, Lexi stayed on the porch for a while deep in thought. She hadn't felt so good in a long time. She sincerely hoped that her mother had convinced Peggy that choosing life over death was always the right answer.

Later that evening, in her room, Lexi closed the

door and prayed earnestly:

"Oh, Father, take care of Peggy. She's very young to have so many serious problems and fears, God. Will you be her comfort and strength? Please assure her of your love for her and your desire to give her a future and a hope. I ask this in Jesus' name, Amen."

Even after crawling into bed and turning off the lamp on her nightstand, it was a long time before Lexi slept. There were still questions that crept into her mind, chasing away the weariness that would have brought her sleep.

Chapter Eleven

"The weather is really weird tonight, isn't it?" Jennifer looked up at the sky as she and her friends sat on the bleachers overlooking the football field. "Creepy, actually."

"It *is* strange," Lexi added. The air was heavy, like a wet blanket on her shoulders. The sky was a steel gray; a storm was brewing.

"You can see lightning in the distance," Jennifer commented. "I sure hope the storm doesn't get here before the game is over. It would be too bad if they had to call it because of weather."

Lexi didn't like the eerie, uncomfortable atmosphere. And the fact that Egg and Binky couldn't seem to quit bickering didn't help her mood either.

"If you think bean sprouts are good for you, then eat them," Binky was saying, "but don't beg Mom to serve them to everyone in the family."

"I'm just thinking of your health, Binky. I wish you wouldn't criticize."

"You're not responsible for my stomach, Egg McNaughton. The only way I'd eat those awful sprouts is with chocolate on them."

"Hey, you two. Break it up! You've been arguing

about something or other all evening." Jennifer poked Egg in the ribs. "Leave your sister alone. She looks healthy enough to me."

"Huh! She's so unhealthy she doesn't even grow. Ever notice how short she is?"

"Are you insulting my height now? Just because you look like a flagpole with no flag doesn't mean I have to be tall and skinny too. All the genes in our family were firmly divided, that's all: you got the tall ones and I got the short ones. Or maybe you're some kind of genetic robber—a bandit or something."

Jennifer rolled her eyes. "It must be the weather."

Lexi agreed. The whole day had felt strange to her. There was static electricity in the air and everyone seemed crankier and more out of sorts than usual.

Even Todd had been quiet, not his normal, pleasant self. Lexi knew that he had been worrying about the upcoming game. The opposing team had some extra big players. Even the quarterback was six feet two inches tall and weighed over two hundred pounds. He made Todd look like a junior high student.

The only bright spot was that Peggy seemed to be coming out of her depression. The conversation with Lexi's mother had been a real turning point for her. It had forced Peggy to look at things in an entirely new light. For the first time in weeks, Lexi wasn't afraid that Peggy might, on the spur of the moment, try to end her own life.

"Here we go, here we go, here we go!" Binky smacked Lexi on the knee.

"Oh, so Egg finally left? He got tired of fighting with you?"

"No, silly, he's the student team manager. I don't know why he sat up here as long as he did. Just wanted to get on my nerves, I guess." Binky stuck out her lower lip. "Everything's so wacky today! I can't explain it."

Everyone turned their attention to the opening kick-off and the game was underway.

"The guys look terrible!" Jennifer blurted after a few plays. "They're making one mistake after another."

It was true. The Cedar River Cougars were fumbling the ball, running into each other, even tripping over their own teammates! It was obvious to Lexi, who didn't know a lot about football, that they were even running the wrong patterns for the plays.

"Todd acts like he's got lead in his shoes tonight," Binky observed. "He's moving so slowly."

Lexi shuddered. "Yeah. I wonder what's wrong?"

"Atmospheric conditions," Jennifer stated flatly. "We're studying meteorology in science class."

"Maybe he *does* have lead in his shoes," Binky quipped.

Lexi made an effort to laugh. She wished she'd just stayed home. Ben and her parents were curled up in front of the TV set with a huge bowl of popcorn when she went out the door. That looked more exciting than sitting out here in this gloomy weather watching the Cedar River guys make fools of themselves.

"Okay, here's an important play now," Jennifer announced. "Watch this."

It was a running play. Todd received the hike and stepped backward, turning at the same time. He extended the football to the running back, who unfortunately wasn't there to carry out the play Todd had called. Unprepared to run or throw the ball, Todd took two steps backward before he was sacked. A mass of equipment-clad humanity piled on top of him.

"He's creamed!" Jennifer gasped.

Binky grabbed Lexi's arm as the three girls stared at the field. "Lexi, why does Todd always take so long to get up?"

"Just give him a minute," Jennifer said impatiently. "He probably got the wind knocked out of him again."

Lexi was silent. She hoped that was all that was the matter, but she couldn't help worrying every time Todd was on the ground. Seconds passed and he remained unmoved. Lexi's gaze switched to the coaches on the sidelines. Coach Derek paced back and forth for a moment and then started across the playing field.

"Get up, Todd. Come on. Get up," Binky was muttering to herself. "Do you think he got knocked out?"

"He got hit pretty hard."

An icy knot of fear was building in Lexi's stomach. *Why isn't he moving?*

The crowd seemed strangely silent and restless. Coach Derek knelt beside Todd. He was speaking to him.

"He must be conscious," Binky said.

"Shhh!" Jennifer ordered, clamping her hand over Binky's mouth.

Lexi felt cold beads of sweat break out on her neck. Something was very wrong. She knew it instinctively. Her hunch was validated when Coach Derek stood up and waved for the paramedics that stood waiting in their usual spot next to the bleachers. After a brief examination, one of them drove the ambulance onto the field and pulled up alongside Todd's still form.

Lexi's fears heightened as a white-coated attendant pulled a steel stretcher from the ambulance and laid it beside Todd. Though her view was partially obscured, Lexi saw the men carefully lift Todd onto the gurney and then push it into the vehicle.

Sometime during the frozen moments that Lexi stood taking in this terrifying scene, she saw Mr. and Mrs. Winston running across the field to see Todd into the ambulance. Mrs. Winston stepped inside, while Mr. Winston remained to speak in agitated tones with Coach Derek.

"I can't see what's going on! What's happening?" Binky fumed.

Lexi was so frightened she felt faint. Her mind whirled and raced with conflicting emotions, until finally as the ambulance moved slowly off the field, red lights flashing and sirens wailing, she felt suddenly energized. She stepped down from her perch and announced that she had to go to him.

Stumbling over students as she scrambled down the bleachers, Lexi virtually flew to the lower level. Just as she reached the bottom, Minda grabbed her arm.

"No, let me go! I have to get to him!" Lexi's voice was panic-stricken.

"I'll drive you to the hospital. I have a car here," Minda offered, with authority.

Lexi nodded, gasping with relief, and followed Minda to the parking lot. Jennifer and Binky trailed closely behind her.

"Could you see what happened from where you were, Minda?" Lexi's voice was so shaky she hardly recognized it.

Minda shook her head. "I saw him get hit and go down. Then all the guys were on top of him. I don't know who hit him. It all happened so fast."

"Do you know if he was unconscious?"

"I don't think so. I could see his eyes fluttering."

"What do you think is wrong with him?" Lexi sank against the seat, feeling waves of terror crash over her.

"He's going to be fine, Lexi. I'm sure he'll be fine." Binky patted Lexi's shoulders. "They have to be careful, you know. They're just taking him to the hospital to check him out."

"Mrs. Winston lost her shoes running across the field," Lexi remembered. "She didn't even go back for them." Somehow that fact seemed important right now.

Minda glanced in the rearview mirror and pressed her foot to the gas pedal. "My dad said he'd take away the car if I got another speeding ticket," Minda explained, "so I can't go any faster than the speed limit, but I'll get you there. Don't worry."

Lexi turned to Minda's profile, outlined in the pale light of the dashboard. "Thanks, Minda. I really appreciate this."

"Hey, he's my friend too. I don't want anything to happen to him either." Since their mutual concern for Peggy, there had been no more hostility between the girls. Now they shared the potent pain of not knowing how badly Todd was injured.

Fortunately a parking spot was open directly across from the hospital's main entrance. Minda pulled in with a screech and the four girls jumped out of the car. Lexi arrived first at the front desk. "Todd Winston. Uh . . . Football. He just came in by ambulance," she blurted.

The receptionist nodded calmly. "They've taken him to emergency, miss. I'm sorry I can't tell you any more, they won't know anything for a while. If you would like to wait—"

"No!" Lexi protested. She felt herself losing control. Taking a deep breath, she said firmly, "I have to see him."

It was Minda who took charge. "Maybe we could wait with his parents. Is there a family waiting room?"

The receptionist looked from Lexi to Minda and nodded. "Down the hall and to the right." She pointed with her pen.

Lexi hurried down the hallway, Minda, Binky and Jennifer trying to keep up with her. The room was empty.

"They must still be with Todd." Binky tried to sound confident. "They'll be here soon. We'll just sit down and wait." She held a chair for Lexi, but she was too nervous to sit. She paced the floor like a caged animal.

"Everything is wrong! Everything. The weather, the game. Todd was out of sync. How could this have happened?"

"We don't even know what happened yet, Lexi,"

Jennifer reminded her. "Try to be calm."

"I hate the smell of hospitals!" Lexi exclaimed. "It reminds me of when Ben was hit by Jerry Randall's car and he almost died." The frightening incident came back to Lexi full force.

"But Ben came out of it just fine, didn't he?" Jennifer asked. "Ben has no after-effects of the accident. It'll be the same with Todd. Wait and see."

The door opened, and Mr. and Mrs. Winston stepped into the room. Lexi felt sick with fear and anticipation. "How is he?"

Mrs. Winston was pale and trembling, unlike the serene, calm individual Lexi had known. "The doctors are still with him," she said. "They're taking more X-rays."

"What is it? Do they know what's wrong yet?" Lexi asked anxiously.

"It appears Todd has suffered a back or neck injury," Mr. Winston said, visibly shaken, but more calm than his wife. "They don't know yet how extensive the damage is."

Back injury? Neck injury? Lexi had studied about them in first-aid classes at school. She'd learned about how to immobilize patients and what could happen if someone made a wrong move. She sat down on a chair with a thud. "Then he could be . . ." She didn't finish the sentence.

The waiting room door flew open and Peggy stood there with a shocked look on her face. "Egg called," she explained. "He's coming over as soon as he can. He wanted me to be here for you. My mother was calling your parents when I left."

Mrs. Winston stood up and put an arm around

Peggy. "I'm glad you're here, Peggy. I'm glad all of you are here. Todd will be happy to know his friends are concerned for him."

Peggy went directly to Lexi and opened her arms. Without a word, Lexi received her embrace. They clung together like two souls who truly understood each other. Neither was a stranger now to the pain known only to those who love deeply.

"It's going to be okay, Lexi. It's going to be okay. Remember how many times you've told me that? And you wanted me to believe you? Now I want you to believe me. I've been . . . praying about it. I really have."

"Oh, Peggy. I'm so frightened. I'm so afraid it's something bad," Lexi whispered.

A nurse came into the room and spoke to Mr. and Mrs. Winston. They followed her into the hall. Now that the girls were alone, Minda started to pace. "Hey," she said, making an effort to lighten the mood, "who called this meeting anyway?"

"Minda drove me to the hospital," Lexi explained to Peggy. "I couldn't move fast enough to ride in the ambulance."

"I wanted to find out what happened to Todd, too," Minda said. "I sure hope he's going to be all right."

Peggy sat down on the couch and looked at her friends. "This is really weird, you know. Hearing that Todd was hurt did something to me."

"What do you mean?" Binky asked, always curious.

"When Egg called and told me that Todd had been injured, it took me back to the day when I found out that Chad had died."

"Oh, Peggy, I'm so sorry," Jennifer began.

Peggy shook her head. "No, it's okay. It convinced me of something that people have been telling me ever since Chad's death. That life is precious. Every minute is valuable and should be used to the fullest. Life isn't disposable—like Chad seemed to think it was. He threw his life away. Hearing about Todd made me realize what a terrible thing suicide is. It's a desperate, hopeless, useless act.

"Lexi knows that lately I've toyed with the idea of taking my own life. She also knows that I've been getting help. But tonight, when I spontaneously reacted to the news of Todd's accident, I knew that I could never take my own life. I realized at that moment that life is too precious. It is to be cherished, treasured, and enjoyed."

The four girls were speechless, amazed at Peggy's insight.

"Lexi, you said something to me that made a big impression. You said that I had a *reason* to live. At first I brushed it off, but the more I thought about it, the more I knew you were right. I've got my family and my friends. I even have an excellent counselor. But best of all, I have God."

Minda was hanging on every word.

"Do you know what God did for me, Lexi? He allowed me to be angry with Him. He let me throw my questions at Him and He didn't back off. He stayed right with me until I found my way through the mess. He didn't change and He didn't move. He just offered His love until I was capable of receiving it.

"I've learned that life is what happens to us. We

can't control that. But we can control how we *react*
to life. Now, after experiencing the feelings I've had
tonight, I know for sure that I want to live."

Peggy blushed. "I'm sorry I've rambled on so, but
it all came so clearly to me tonight when I was driving down here. I know you're worried about Todd,
Lexi, but I thought it might help if you didn't have
to worry about me anymore."

Lexi stood up. It was her turn to hold out her arms
to her friend. The two embraced until they wept. "I'm
so glad you've chosen life," Lexi murmured.

"Not only that, I've chosen to enjoy it," Peggy responded.

Lexi looked over Peggy's shoulder at Minda. She
was crying too. It was hard to believe. She wasn't the
Minda they had all known.

Lexi sighed deeply. "You're all right, Peggy, and
I know Todd's going to be all right, too."

Suddenly confident and knowing what needed to
be done next, Lexi released Peggy and took Minda's
hand. "I think we've got some praying to do. We need
to pray for Todd's recovery, and we also should give
thanks for what God has done for Peggy."

The others nodded silently and joined hands. Lexi
began with praise and thanks for Peggy and for the
knowledge that she was going to make it, but even
as she prayed she wondered anxiously about Todd.
Was he really going to be all right?

————

Lexi and her friends have survived the ordeal of
their classmate Chad's death. Now they face new les-

sons and challenges with Todd's football injury. Will they come out on top? Will Lexi's faith stand the test?

Find the answers in Cedar River Daydreams Number 14, *Second Chance*.

A Note From Judy

I'm glad you're reading *Cedar River Daydreams*! I hope I've given you something to think about as well as a story to entertain you. If you feel you have any of the problems that Lexi and her friends experience, I encourage you to talk with your parents, a pastor, or a trusted adult friend. There are many people who care about you!

Also, I enjoy hearing from my readers, so if you'd like to write, my address is:

Judy Baer
Bethany House Publishers
6820 Auto Club Road
Minneapolis, MN 55438

Please include an <u>addressed, stamped envelope</u> if you would like an answer. Thanks.